FEAR IN THE GLE

"Chosen and favoured and gifted, they say. Oh, child, be careful!" said Winnag the wise woman.

Bel's determination to improve her family's fortunes has put her in danger. It has brought her to the notice of the priests of the glen. Now they are seeking a sacrifice and Bel is the Chosen One.

She is sure that Columba, the gentle yet powerful lord from Ireland, will be able to help. But no one knows where he is, and time is running out . . .

FEAR
IN THE
GLEN

Jenny Robertson

A LION PAPERBACK
Oxford · Batavia · Sydney

Published by
Lion Publishing plc
Sandy Lane West, Oxford, England
ISBN 0 7459 1874 3
Lion Publishing Corporation
1705 Hubbard Avenue, Batavia, Illinois 60510, USA
ISBN 0 7459 1874 3
Albatross Books Pty Ltd
PO Box 320, Sutherland, NSW 2232, Australia
ISBN 0 7324 0209 3

First edition published by Scripture Union in 1984
under the title *Where Red Deer Run*.
This revised edition first published 1990

British Library Cataloguing in Publication Data
(Applied for)

Library of Congress Cataloging in Publication Data
(Applied for)

Printed and bound in Great Britain
by Cox and Wyman Ltd, Reading

CONTENTS

Some of the old customs mentioned in this book are still observed today, not least the feast of Samhain, which we now call Hallowe'en. You can still climb the rocky hill of Dunadd, where King Connail set his High Fort. You can walk beside the burn where Bel picked rowans, as well as the river, where you might see a heron. And although it has a different name, you can visit the Maiden's Ring with its ancient stones. The Celtic Church of Columba and his monks has long since disappeared, but their prayers have never been forgotten, and are being rediscovered and loved, while Columba's green isle of Iona has become again a place of pilgrimage and healing.

J.R.

1
BEL'S QUESTIONS

Being the oldest girl in a family of five children, Bel was always kept busy. She had to help her mother spin wool, dye it and weave long threads into cloth for the family to wear. She had to help when ale was brewed and bread was baked, and she had to teach her little sisters so that they could help too.

So most of her days were spent inside the family's one-roomed hut, where an iron cooking pot simmered on the fire which never went out. Herbs were dried in the rafters, bread was baked on stones around the fire, and at night the family all slept together, huddled close to the banked-up glow.

But sometimes Bel managed to run out into the wind and the sun. She went up the hill behind their homestead. Often deer rose from the bracken and bounded away from her. In the autumn months Bel's family would hear the sound of antlers clashing together as the stags fought.

Bel loved the shy deer with their red-brown coats and longed to fondle their soft noses, but they never let her come close enough.

"I would never hurt you," Bel would whisper, "but you always run away."

Her father and the other men hunted the deer with shaggy hounds brought by ship from Ireland. They used javelins, throwing sticks and spears, and if they managed to kill a deer the family would eat venison. Bel ate her share too. She was always too hungry to refuse, but she hated to think that a deer had been killed.

They wore shoes made from deer hide and used thongs of hide to bind their long hair and belt their clothes. Bel's father sometimes wore soft deerskin trousers.

"Men always have to kill," thought Bel, but she knew too that women cooked and ate the meat men killed, and when they sat at their sewing they used needles of bone.

"I'm glad deer can run fast because it keeps them safe," she thought, "even though I can never come close enough to stroke them."

The other place Bel went to, besides the hill, was the burn* which tumbled over boulders, rushing to the river which wound across their glen. Bel liked the river too, but she didn't have enough free time to go there often. But she went to the burn every day with her sisters to fetch water. The family washed their clothes there too.

The water in the burn was clear and sweet, and once, when Bel was sitting beside the burn, a saying formed itself in her head. It came almost by itself, but the more it floated around in her mind

* burn = stream

the more it troubled her. The words flowed into a little rhyme:

Why are the deer so swift and fleet?
Why does burn water taste so sweet?

She knew the answer to the first part, of course. The deer had to be swift and fleet to run away from danger, otherwise they would easily be killed. But what about the second part? After all, the sea, she knew, was salt. You could die of thirst at sea, her father said.

Bel pondered the problem as she filled two leather bottles with burn water and scooped up handfuls to drink.

Rain water was sweet too. The family collected it in a barrel, but it soon tasted stale once it had been standing. They washed with it, using an iron ladle to pour the water over their hands and feet and long hair.

The thing about rainwater was that you didn't have to carry it. There was nearly always enough of it too, but in times of drought it was amazing how quickly the burn dwindled to a trickle, so that dirt got into the leather bottles. Then, if there still wasn't any rain, a whisper soon began to go round, like the rustle of the wind in dry leaves. The whispered word was sacrifice, which meant that someone would be chosen to die.

"Why?" Bel wondered, and that second question joined the first one in her mind and tumbled around, confusing her.

She knew someone who might tell her the answer. It was Winnag, the wise woman, who was very old. People said she had fairy blood in her.

"Whether that's so or not, it's certain that she is descended from the dark people who lived in our glen long ago and built the stone rings here," said Bel's mother. "You can't trust those people. Winnag is a bearer of ill-luck and you children must never go near her."

"But if everyone thinks that, old Winnag won't have any friends," argued Bel.

"Oh yes, she's got friends," said her mother, darkly, "and they're not the kind we want to have dealings with."

Whatever that meant, it can't have been good, because as she spoke Bel's mother touched a lucky bone she wore round her neck and made a sign to ward off evil.

Just the same, Bel's question bothered her so much that one day in early May when she was taking their lambs down the glen to share her uncle's pasture, she called in at Winnag's tumbledown hut to ask the old woman if she knew the answer.

Winnag's friends must indeed be the sort it was better not to know because her hut was in ruins and her fire had almost no fuel to feed it. The old woman too was in rags. She was so thin you could see all her bones. Her head shone through scant wisps of grey hair. A scrawny cat lay by her fire, thick with fleas.

"It's dark and smelly here," thought Bel. "Perhaps I should go home after all. But if I do I'll never know why there are all those whispers in our glen."

Dirt in our leather bottles means we get ill. Babies and old folk die. That's what the whisperers said. *We must make a sacrifice. The Chosen One will die.*

Bel shivered. "Winnag might know how to help our glen," she thought. "She belongs here. Her people were here before my father and other warriors sailed from Ireland with the king in the High Fort, and before the priests in the Maiden's Ring, even though they came to the glen a very long time ago. Mother says Winnag brings ill luck. People also say Winnag is old and wise. I'm going to speak to Winnag even if her hut is smelly and her cat's got fleas."

So Bel stepped inside Winnag's hut.

The thatch of bracken and turf was in holes and sunlight filtered through. Winnag sat on the ground, her bony fingers on her thin knees. She smiled at Bel, showing stained wide-spaced teeth.

"Come in, come in," she invited, as though visitors came by every day. "Welcome in, dearie. It's a beautiful day."

Bel nodded. Grown-ups always talked about the weather, but somehow she had expected Winnag to talk in spells or be busy with magic.

"All alone, are you?" Winnag went on. "You'll be the wee girl from the homestead up the hill."

"I'm ten. I'm the oldest in my family," Bel started to protest, but Winnag went on talking.

13

Her chin wobbled. Her face was as bony as a skeleton's with so little hair to hide her skull, and Bel drew back from the smell of decay which clung to the old woman. Her questions seemed very silly now, and she didn't think that Winnag was as wise as everyone said. She was just a poor old woman after all, in spite of all the stories which had grown up about her.

"This heat puts me in mind of the days of the drought," Winnag was saying. "What a terrible time that was! The barley sickened and the corn was rotten. That's always bad."

Bel nodded. "Let's hope it doesn't happen again," she began, but Winnag went on talking.

"Fires spread quickly when there's drought. The whole moorland blazes, and the corn turns black on the stalk. No rain means bad harvests, and bad harvests mean hunger."

And now Bel felt frightened. Why did the old woman keep speaking of ill, almost as though she wanted it to happen? Perhaps her mother was right to call Winnag a bearer of ill-luck. Bel drew back a step trying to go, but the question which puzzled her so much forced itself into words.

"Why, Winnag, why?" she burst out.

Winnag looked at Bel curiously. "Why, what?" she asked.

"Oh, Winnag, I don't know," said Bel. "So many things worry me. I came here hoping you might be able to help me."

"Now what made you think that?" asked Winnag.

"I don't know . . . people say . . ." Bel shifted from one foot to the other and turned away miserably. "I'd better go home now."

"No, don't go yet. You'll stay for a drink. I was out picking primroses." Old Winnag got herself creaking to her feet as she spoke. "You'll like broth made of primroses. Look, I've some here, all ready. Children always like it. I did too, when I was young with my sisters. Do you have sisters at home, dearie?"

"Three sisters and one brother," said Bel.

"Well, now, that's a nice family," said Winnag, pouring her concoction into a cracked beaker. "Here we are now! My, my, it's quite a party we're having! I'm glad I picked primroses. But sit down now, my dear."

Bel sat on the dry earth floor, avoiding the cat. The beaker was filthy and Winnag's broth didn't look nearly as good as her mother's. Bel sipped it, trying to look as if she was enjoying it.

"It's very nice broth," she said politely, just as her mother did when they went visiting relations in the High Fort or in homesteads across the glen.

Winnag smiled, pleased, and lowered herself to the ground. "Now, what were your questions, my dear?" she asked.

"Oh, I don't know . . ." Bel rocked the beaker between her cupped fingers, trying to shake roots, leaves and pieces of powdery petal out of the way.

"Something is troubling you," said Winnag.

And Bel thought to herself grimly, "Yes — how

15

to drink your horrible broth. We always strain ours through a cloth first." But she didn't say so. Instead, the problem burst out of her. "Winnag, why must there be so much death? And why does the water in our burn taste sweet? The river water isn't sweet, although salmon swim there. My brother Derril goes with the other boys to catch them. And the hazelnuts grow beside the river, but, just the same, the water isn't sweet, Derril says. And the sea isn't sweet, either."

"No," Winnag agreed, "the sea is a terrible thing, child. It brings fighting men in ships. You can drown in the sea."

"Oh, I think the sea is beautiful!" exclaimed Bel. "There are seals there, Winnag. I love seals. We go to the sea sometimes to get seal oil for our lamps and sealskins too. I feel the same way about the seals as I do about deer. Why do they have to be killed?"

"You've said why yourself," Winnag pointed out. "For oil and skins, and the deer for their hides and their meat."

Bel shifted on the ground and put her beaker down. She really couldn't drink any more. "Why, Winnag, why?" she asked. "Why do animals and people, even children have to die?" And now the whispered word *sacrifice* echoed inside her thoughts, and she said, "And why do they talk about a sacrifice . . ."

Winnag stared at her. "There is always death, my dear, always," she said. "men bring death in their ships across the sea. Priests offer death in

16

their temples. The gods demand death so that the corn will grow and the rivers will flow. Don't worry about it. Just think instead that the water in your burn is very sweet. May it always be so, dearie, and when you taste it you'll maybe remember old Winnag and come and see me again one day."

"Do many people come to visit you?" asked Bel, but she regretted the question because Winnag didn't answer and Bel guessed that her reply might well be "no".

In the silence which followed Bel said, "Thank you for the primrose broth, Winnag."

She got up to go. Winnag hadn't been able to answer her questions, but talking the problem over had cleared her mind a little.

"When you next come I'll tell you a story," promised Winnag. "Then perhaps you'll understand better how it was that the sea, the death-dealer, became salt."

"Tell me now," said Bel.

"No," said Winnag, "you've been here long enough."

And now it was Bel's turn to stare. Did Winnag know that mothers forbade their children to see her, that she was blamed whenever there was trouble in the glen?

"Thank you for helping me with my questions," she said, "and for the primrose broth," she added again, hoping Winnag wouldn't be offended when she saw all the broth Bel had left in her cup.

"Thank you for your visit, my dear," Winnag said.

All the way home Bel went over their conversation in her mind. She wished she could tell her mother about it, that she could say, "Winnag is just a lonely old woman. She certainly isn't evil. And the primrose broth she makes is horrible, not like yours at all." But her mother would only say that she had been bewitched. And Bel herself couldn't be sure that she hadn't, but not in the sense that her mother might mean.

2

THE BOY WITH THE IRON COLLAR

"There are three things that are good," sang Bel's mother as she ground barley to flour with heavy stones.

"Hazelnuts, rowans and gorse," chanted Bel in reply, taking her turn at the stones.

Bel's mother wearily pushed back her heavy loose hair. A gold armband gleamed on her bare upper arm. It was very old. She had worn it the day she got married and along with the carved kist* which held her stores it was her most treasured possession.

Bel's mother came from a family which had belonged to the glen for centuries, though not for as long as Winnag's people. They followed the ways of the priests in the Maiden's Ring. Bel's father's family, however, had come from Ireland with their warrior king who conquered the High Fort at the end of the glen. So now Bel's glen became part of the kingdom of Dalriada. The Kings of Dalriada followed the Christian faith, but it hadn't yet spread to the people of the glen. They spoke a different language too. Bel's brother Derril and the three little girls, Elir, Genann and Mooreen all had

* kist = large box

Irish names, but Bel's own name came from her mother's British tongue. Sometimes Bel wished she had an Irish name too. At other times she was glad to have the name from the older language.

"My name belongs here," she would often say, "like the rhymes you sing," she would add, for her mother loved to sing. "And like the hazelnuts, the rowans and gorse."

"And the salmon, the hind and her doe," smiled her mother.

But these warm days her mother didn't sing or smile much. Bel supposed it was because she was having a baby. Yet surely that would make her mother happy?

"I'm tired. I don't feel well," her mother said. "Go on with the grinding, Bel, and let's sing some more charms."

"Land of honey, of blossom and heather," began Bel, and her little sisters joined in, "Land of nutbushes, dear land of the hills . . ."

"I shall give you three rings," Bel went on. Her sisters, Elir, Genann and Mooreen, who didn't know the rest of this rhyme, listened with interest while her mother straightened with a sign.

Stones standing in rings,
rings on burn water which spills
over our glen, guarded on all sides
by circling hills.

"May they guard me and my baby," said her

mother. "And yet that's a chancy rhyme, Bel, for two reasons."

"What are they then?' asked Bel.

"The stones standing in rings guard the worship of our glen, but they are built on death, and sometimes the dead demand sacrifice," her mother explained, and now her hands were round the lucky bone she always wore.

Bel shivered. There it was again: death and sacrifice, but her rhyme had seemed to her full of sound of burn water, and burn water, as Winnag had agreed, was sweet.

"What's the other reason?" she asked.

"Jewelled rings of rich red gold are worn by kings, but slaves have rings of iron round their necks. Royal rings and pride of kings may become the shame of thralls*," her mother said. "Go and pick me a spray of rowan, Bel, and we'll put it high on the wall against the ill-luck in your charm."

Bel hurried outside. The sun dazzled her after the smokey room.

Rowans, heavy with creamy blossom, grew beside the burn. Bel hurried to pick some blossom, but drew back in surprise as she saw someone there.

It was a slave boy, with a thrall's iron collar round his neck.

"What are you doing here?" shouted Bel. "Go away." But really she was trying to drive away all the ill-chance her mother feared.

It was not for a slave to answer back or disobey. He picked up a heavy load beside him, wrapped in a piece of cloth.

* thralls = slaves

21

"No, don't go yet," said Bel. "Let me touch your collar. Iron drives away fairies and their evil dance."

So the boy stood still, holding his heavy bundle and Bel came up to him and put her hot fingers on the iron collar round the slave's unwashed neck.

"Does it hurt" she asked, noticing sores.

He nodded. "It makes me sweat," he said huskily. And then with a kind of bitter mockery he added, "Aren't you afraid that a slave's collar will bring you ill-luck?"

"Why should it? It's iron after all, and that's the main thing," said Bel.

"It's my bad luck," said the slave, "and there's no power on earth can change that."

She drew back, afraid. "Pick me some blossom," she said. "I came out so quickly I forgot to bring a knife."

He set down his bundle again, pulled out a knife and picked Bel some blossom. She took it and held out a sprig for him. "For good luck," she said, and thrust it into the pin which fastened the neck of his tunic.

"May it bring you luck too," he said, and started to go.

"Where do you live?" asked Bel.

"Beside the stone circle called the Maiden's Ring," he answered, naming the very same unlucky thing which had brought Bel out here for blossoms. The Maiden's Ring stood amidst woods beyond the river which flowed through the middle of the glen, and she had just been singing about "stones standing in rings".

"I've been there," she said. "The priests live in the temple close by the Ring. Next month will be the Midsummer Solstice. My mother and the girls and I will go to the Ring for the ceremony.'

"Perhaps I shall see you then," said the boy, "but you won't want to notice me."

"Of course I will," said Bel. "You've been to our burn and picked blossom for us. What's your name?"

"Coll," said the boy. "I belong to a priest called Wyn."

"I'm Bel," she told him. "I live in the homestead over there. My father lives with us, of course, but whenever the king needs him he sharpens his weapons and goes off to war."

"There's a new warrior in the High Fort these days," said Coll.

"Is there? I hadn't heard," said Bel.

"He's not a warrior really," said Coll, "but he's very powerful. He wins wars without any weapons."

"That's impossible," retorted Bel.

"Not for him," said Coll. "He's a very great lord, but he's become a monk now — that's someone who spends his time praying and helping people," he added. "He's called Columba, which means a dove. I wish I belonged to him and not to Wyn, but he hasn't any slaves."

"Oh?" said Bel. "I must go now. My mother wants her rowan blossoms. Good luck again."

"I need it," said Coll, "but I don't know where I'll find it."

"Perhaps the rowan blossom will help?"

"Maybe," he said, picking up his bundle again. He went striding away downhill and Bel hurried in with her blossoms and the news that she had found the things she had mentioned in her song.

But her story made her mother very angry. "Bad luck is sure to come," she kept saying. "I shall go to the temple beside the Ring and offer a sacrifice. You must come with me, Bel."

"But how will you get there, over all the rough ground?" Bel asked.

"I'll manage it somehow, even if I have to drag myself there. It's all your fault, Bel! Bad enough seeing the slave, after your rhyme, but why did you have to talk to him? If you hadn't done that we wouldn't be talking about the Maiden's Ring."

"I didn't know. I'm sorry," said Bel. "I thought I'd touch his collar, that's all."

"Touch a slave's collar! Whatever for?"

"It's iron, isn't it?' said Bel.

"Iron, oh yes, it's iron, all right."

"Well then," began Bel.

"I thought you knew better. A free person never touches a slave."

"Not a slave, just his collar. It makes his neck all sore," said Bel, but that shocked her mother still more. "You'll bring bad luck on us all for sure," she said.

Bel, remembering her visit to Winnag, which

24

she didn't feel able to tell her mother about, began to think, in the troubles which lay ahead, that her mother had been right. Either Winnag or even Bel herself had become the bearer of ill.

For still no rain came, and sickness spread through the glen, even though Bel's mother filled the house with creamy rowan blossom and other lucky things. She went to the temple too, taking Bel with her. Bel looked for Coll, but he was nowhere to be seen as they offered their sacrifice and listened while a priest chanted prayers from a part of the wooden temple where no woman might go.

Through the richly carved archways Bel could glimpse the circle of standing stones known as the Maiden's Ring. The sun slanted between the stones sending out a radius of black shadows. Bel watched the shadows tremble as clouds drifted across the sun. Then her mother got up to go. Bel stood up too. Her mother pulled off her gold armband and held it out to the richly dressed priest to pay for their sacrifice. And then Bel understood just how much harm she had done, all unwitting. She wished she could undo it somehow. It was terrible that her mother had had to part with the precious armband. Without it her arm was white and the skin was dented in, but it slowly filled out and the mark faded as time went on.

And as summer wore on the troubles mounted. The first thing to happen was that, soon after their long rough walk over the moorland back from the temple, the baby which had been growing inside Bel's mother began to be born, far too soon. Women from the homesteads across the burn and over the river came to help, but when the baby, a boy, came, he was born dead.

It was stifling hot in the room. Soiled rushes smouldered on the fire. The women talked, their voices rising and falling. Bel's father and Derril were banned from the house. Sometimes one of the women remembered about the little girls and poured them some broth or gave them some bread to eat. Mostly they forgot about Bel who sat in the shadows, dumbly watching.

"Why?" her heart cried within her. "Why is there so much suffering? Why was the baby born dead?"

The women moved from the rushes where her mother lay to the fire and back. Herbs were boiled. Her mother had a fever. Her mother was ill, they said. Maybe her mother was going to die.

"And it's all my fault," thought Bel. "I went to Winnag, although I knew my mother wouldn't like it. I sang unlucky rhymes. I touched a slave's collar. What can I do now that the baby is dead."

Slowly a plan formed itself in her head, but it was so difficult and dangerous Bel had no idea how she would ever be able to carry it out.

3

WATCHER BY THE WATER

At first light of day, as soon as the plan formed in her mind, Bel went back to Winnag.

"I know Mother wouldn't like it," she thought, a bit uncomfortably, "but Winnag belongs to our glen. And I've got no one else to talk to."

The old woman was alone in her hut. There was no sign of the cat.

"I have no broth," said Winnag, "but you are welcome, Bel."

"I didn't come for any broth," said Bel. "I wanted to speak to you, Winnag."

"Indeed and I'm glad," said Winnag. "For I see you are full of troubles."

"My mother thinks I shouldn't come here and speak to you," Bel began, and Winnag's face darkened.

"What weapons have deer when hunters invade the hill?" she asked. "What weapons had my people when conquerors came long ago with iron swords and drove us from the glen? Only some of us stayed, little and poor. We do no one harm. Your mother's folk need our wisdom in times of ill, but there's no love between us."

"You told me just now I was welcome," said Bel.

"And so you are, Bel, but old hurts go deep."

"So do new troubles," thought Bel. Aloud she said, "Please listen to me, Winnag, no matter what my mother's people have done. My mother is ill. She may be dying. And our baby died. I've got to do something to turn ill luck away. That's why I've come to see you."

"Ah, Bel of the questing heart, lass of the sore troubles, let there be no hardness between us. You say you want to turn ill luck away?"

"Yes. I'm going to the Maiden's Ring, Winnag. It's the only way I know."

"All alone, Bel?"

"I must," said Bel. "There's no one to go with me."

"No, lass, it's too far for old Winnag, and the priests of the Ring don't like me or my old ways, but it's a long journey for you also, Bel."

Bel nodded. The Maiden's Ring had seemed far enough away when she went with her mother over moorland criss-crossed by burns and the brown river which wound its way past the High Fort and down to the sea. And if, like Bel, you seldom strayed further than the burn by the homestead or the hill behind it, the Ring and the priests' Temple close by it was a considerable distance indeed.

And of course, to go to a place so old and mysterious as the Maiden's Ring, a place of good and ill, of celebration and death, was something no adult would dream of doing, unless the need was great.

But Bel's need was very great and so she said, "I know it's a long way, but I must go, Winnag. Besides, it's almost the time of the Midsummer Solstice . . ."

"When there is hardly any dark," Winnag nodded her agreement. "So you'll have the day time and the long light evening to journey there and back. Well, it's a brave lassie you are right enough, Bel of the sad eyes, and Winnag wishes you well. Take this knife, and cut yourself a spray of leaves from the rowan tree, fresh and green as they are, and lay them on the stones as an offering from Winnag. And here's a piece of scone for you and a small bottle of water. Go now, my dear, and remember, no matter what the past enmity between your folk and mine, old Winnag wishes you well."

So Bel set off alone, glad of the old woman's good wishes as she followed the course of the burn down towards the long peaceful levels of the glen.

People had lived here for centuries: Winnag's people, her mother's people, and now themselves. Centuries. Her head reeled. She had lived only ten years. Her mind could hardly grasp the long reach of time back into the past, yet it was comforting to think that her glen had provided shelter, food and safety for so many years. It made her feel safe too.

But of course the glen had seen death as well. Stretching along the glen were five huge grassy mounds where the dead lay. And near the mounds were the stones: circles of stones like the Maiden's Ring, carved with markings no one could fathom, guarded the graves of people long since dead. And the stones themselves, it was whispered, were built on the bones of dead children who had been offered to the gods as a sacrifice.

Here in the glen where pasture and cornfield kept the living safe, the dead, as those who whispered the words *Chosen One* knew, sometimes demanded a sacrifice, even though, every year as the lean short days and lengthening nights began, the dead were remembered in a special feast called Samhain.

But sometimes extra special efforts were needed, and Bel was making one now, to try to ward off from her family the power of the dead her unlucky rhymes seem to have unleashed. And although many folk beside Bel's mother would have agreed that touching Coll's iron collar and visiting Winnag were chancy things which also brought harm, in her heart Bel felt that such sayings were wrong.

"No matter what people say, Coll and Winnag have both wished me well," she thought, as she picked her way across bogs and boulders, wading with difficulty thigh deep through the cold water of the swift-flowing river. She had to hold her woollen, sleeveless dress very high, and emerged shaking with cold and fright. There was a ford higher up. Her mother and she had used it before, but Bel wasn't sure exactly where it was. She had chosen what had seemed to her the most direct route and now was learning that short cuts are often not the best way after all.

But eventually, towards noon, she arrived at the Maiden's Ring.

"If stones could talk what stories they would tell," she said, half-aloud, talking to give herself courage, but her voice sounded strange as she stood all alone close beside the wide ring of carved stones.

She was hungry but it seemed wrong to eat her scone here. Slowly, fearfully she came closer to the stones. They towered about her, like giants. In the noon sunlight they had only stunted shadows, and Bel was glad, almost as though the shadows and not the stones had the power.

Even though her feet were bare it felt wrong to be treading here, yet she kept on walking until she stood right on the very edge of the stone circle. She looked round. No one was in sight, but the temple and the enclosure where the priests lived were both very close. She could hear the clatter of cooking pots, the sound of voices and the pounding of grinding stones. A dog barked. There was a good smell of cooking too. It was said that the priests ate well, better even than the king.

But here, among the old carved stones, was sunlight and stillness. Bel walked steadily forward. In the very centre of the ring was a smaller ring, surrounding a grave. Bel took out the spray of rowan leaves she had cut with Winnag's knife.

They were withered now, but she put them beside the grave. "That's from Winnag," she said. Then she reached out and laid her hands on the stones on either side of her. They were rough and warm beneath her fingers.

"Stones, guard my family," she prayed aloud. 'Keep the dead from our hearth. My mother is dying. Bring her back to life.'

Would the stones hear? Would they answer? Was there some power within them which might bring life and not death?

"Answer me, stones," demanded Bel. "I've walked barefoot here to pray to you. Don't just stand and do nothing!"

It occurred to her that perhaps the stones demanded a price. She remembered how her mother had parted with her armband.

"I haven't got anything to give you," she thought, but then she remembered the scone Winnag had given her. She hesitated. She was hungry. She could still smell the priest's dinner. Since the start of her mother's illness Bel had eaten no cooked food. The women had been too busy, making medicines and brewing up potions while they sang old charms.

Still, Bel knew she would have to pay the price. Prayer could never be made without sacrifice. But would it count if she made the offering herself, or should she not find one of the priests and ask if he would help her?

"Perhaps I'd better do that, like my mother did," she thought. "What was the name of Coll's priest, the one he belongs to? Wyn! That's it. I'll go and find him."

She hurried away from the stone circle towards the priest's enclosure, but doubts gnawed at her. "They'll only laugh at me," she thought. "Priests want silver and gold, not pieces of barley scone. Besides, they only eat bread made from fine wheat flour themselves." She hesitated, walking more slowly, trying to make up her mind, but within her heart she knew she had to go through with this no matter if she got laughed at or even ran into danger.

Her bare feet trod rough stones carefully. Slaves hurried to and fro. No one noticed her. She turned towards the wooden temple where slaves crouched on the steps, waiting for someone. As Bel started to climb the imposing stairway they jumped to attention. A richly dressed priest, his shaved forehead hidden beneath a crown of white owl feathers, came up the steps towards them. Bel waited till he drew level with her, then, too nervous to remember any of the correct greetings, she blurted out hurriedly, "Is your name Wyn?"

He looked at her in astonishment and paused, his slaves stopping too, and now something surprising happened. Instead of brushing aside the dishevelled girl-child, he bent towards her. "Yes, I am Wyn," he said. "What brings you here?"

"I don't know," Bel began. The answer plainly didn't impress him, but she went on hastily. "The powers of life and death both together, I think. You see, there's a power which makes burn water sweet and another which stole life from my baby brother. And now my mother is ill. I had to do something, so I went to the Maiden's Ring to pray for her life. . . .'

She wanted to go on and explain that she had a piece of bread to offer, but Wyn thrust out a jewelled hand.

"To the Maiden's Ring?" he said. "Alone? A child like you?"

"I'm the oldest in my family," Bel began, but then she admitted, "Yes, I was scared, but I would have gone at midnight if I had needed to."

"Yes," Wyn said slowly, "I believe you would."

"It wasn't so bad just now because there are hardly any shadows," Bel went on, but Wyn interrupted her.

"Be careful. Some things are better not spoken of," he said, and his voice sounded hard.

"I'm sorry," said Bel. "I didn't know."

"No, how could you?" And now his voice sounded far away and his eyes seemed to look right through her. "How could you?" he repeated, "yet I believe you are favoured, one of the Gifted Ones . . ."

What did that mean? And why was Wyn looking at her as though he could see right inside her?

"So, you went to the Ring?" Wyn repeated, moving slowly up the steps towards the temple, followed by his slaves. "And now you have dared venture inside our enclosure."

"I'm sorry," Bel said again, and by dint of quick climbing, she kept pace with Wyn and tried to explain, "I don't want my mother to die. I had to make an offering, but all I have with me is this piece of barley scone."

To her relief Wyn didn't laugh at her. By now they were at the top of the steps. Heavy doors blocked the entrance to the temple and over the top of them were rows of shrivelled heads, whose owners had either died in battle or had been sacrificed. The king in the High Fort forbade human sacrifice but the priests followed old ways. It was believed that heads stuck up high were immensely holy and powerful and that they could speak out about matters concerning life and death, and especially at Samhain Feast.

Wyn bowed to the heads and then went on speaking to Bel. "There's no need to make an offering now, child. It's plain you've been specially chosen. What is your name and where do you live?"

Bel told him. "Will the stones answer my prayer even without the bread?" she persisted, because she had to find out whether her mother would get better or not.

Wyn's jewelled fingers spread wide in the sun. "Will you never stop asking questions?" he demanded. "I told you, your prayer has been accepted and you may go home now. But whether your prayer has been answered in the way you hope, who can say?"

"You mean . . . my mother may . . . ?" Tears came to Bel's eyes. What was the use of praying then, she thought angrily, if after all her effort and daring her mother still died?

The priest made an impatient gesture with his soft fingers. "Do you want me to stand here all day answering your questions? I said, you can go. I've favoured you with my attention long enough." He turned away, but then he paused and, looking back over his shoulder, he asked, "Tell me one thing" How did you know my name?"

"One of your thralls called Coll," Bel began, but regretted instantly mentioning the boy's name, for Wyn's face darkened.

"That useless runaway! He disappeared yesterday. Oh, not without telling the rest. 'I'm going to hear the monk from Ireland,' he said. 'Do my work for me till I get back.' What an idea! He'll be beaten when he next turns up. Be off with you, child."

Bel obeyed at once. "I don't like Wyn's voice," she thought, "and I don't want him to beat Coll. Coll said he'd rather belong to the Irish monk Columba than to Wyn. But Columba doesn't keep slaves. So where else can Coll go? No one else will ever take in a runaway, and especially not one who belongs to the priests."

Bel's heard was very heavy as she went slowly down the flight of steps, but because she was still hungry she sat down by the river, well away from the temple, to eat her bread. The river was shallower here and flowed more gently. A heron flew up from the bank. Normally Bel would have been thrilled at the sight of the grey bird with its widespread wings. She was too tired and too disappointed to pay any attention to it at all. She curled up on the bank and closed her eyes.

She must have dozed in the warm sunshine. The next thing she knew was the sound of singing: men's voices mainly, and the words they sang were unknown to her.

Feeling thirsty she reached down to scoop up some of the brown brackish water.

"Oh!" she exclaimed, and drew back.

A man stood on the bank opposite, a tall man with the sun behind him and a baby in his arms. If it hadn't been for the baby Bel would have thought him a warrior, or even a prince, but then he saw that his feet under his long robe were bare, and instead of having his hair twisted into braids as the warriors did, the front of his head had been shaved, like a priest's.

He held the baby very tenderly as he bent to the running water. "In the Name of the Father all-powerful, the Son all-loving and the Spirit all-wisdom," he said. Then he splashed water on the baby's head. He brushed the water away and made a mark with his thumb on the baby's forehead. "I mark the cross on your brow. May God the Father walk with you, may God the Son guard you and God the Spirit pour out light upon you."

"Amen," the people said, and Bel noticed that besides the men who had been singing, and who were dressed in the same style as the man with the baby, were people from the glen, including some thralls. And among them she saw Coll.

"Then that man must be the Irish monk, Columba," Bel thought. "He's the man Coll says fights without weapons."

Columba walked back up the bank and handed the baby back to its mother, while the monks chanted their hymns.

"These are the Three Guarding Ones," they sang, and Bel, listening, thought, "Winnag will be pleased that Columba and his monks are guarding our glen. I must tell Mother too — oh, but I wish I could tell Columba about all the unchancy sayings and troubles, about our baby and how ill Mother is . . ."

But the monks were still singing. Their voices rose and fell like the sound of the sea, and among these Irish monks were men from Bel's glen. Their words sang in her head:

These are the Three Guarding Ones,
Father, Spirit and the Son.
Be ever with us, Lord, we pray:
each noon, each dark, each break of day.

"Come now," Columba said, and one of the thralls stepped forward. Columba took his hand and led him down to the river bank. The thrall knelt, bending his head and Columba scooped up water again, saying the same words as before; only this time, as the man got to his feet, Columba, who, Coll had said, was a very great lord, kissed him, while the chanting went on.

Bel watched astonished. What lord was this, who walked barefoot, handled babies and kissed thralls? But now Coll was walking forward, and Bel saw that his face above the iron collar was quiet and glad.

She watched him kneel beside the river and bend his head beneath the pouring out of the water which trickled down beneath his slave's collar. Then Coll too received Columba's kiss and the monks stopped singing while Columba spoke.

"I have marked you with the cross," he said, "and now you belong to the King of the Kings, for whose sake I have come here, east of Ireland. I am his thrall. Go and serve him too, wherever he may place you. It won't be easy, I know. Darkness and old powers and wrong longings strive together, but Christ our Lord will help you, and now in his name I bless you."

He stretched out his hand, brown and bare of jewels. He made a shape of a cross in the air, and they knelt, praying beside the singing river, while the baby slept in its mother's arms.

And then, as they moved away, Columba spoke across the river bank to Bel.

"Receive the blessings of the Most High too, little watcher by the bank," he said, making the shape of the cross again with his bare brown hand. "May God the Father always guard you, God the Son always protect you, and God the

Spirit always bless you, and all within your house."

Instinctively Bel stretched out her hands, as though she could reach out and hold those words of protection. "Always," Columba had just prayed three times and, "All within your house". These words seemed important to Bel, but already Columba had turned away, and Col followed him closely. Bel wished she could warn him about the beating in store for him, but the river ran between them. Columba's voice had carried clearly, but hers would be lost in the river noise. And by the time she had waded across they were well away. Bel didn't like to try to catch them up. She made her way home to find that her mother was sitting by the fire, still very weak, but over the worst of her fever. The women had all gone, except for one friend who was busy cooking a dinner which smelt very good.

"Where have you been, Bel?" her mother scolded.

4

WINNAG'S STORY

As soon as she could Bel hurried back to find Winnag and tell her that her mother was better. And, of course, she had to ask her the question which had troubled her ever since she had received Columba's blessing at the river bank and gone home to find her mother recovering.

"What do you think, Winnag?" "What do I think?" asked Winnag. "What you are asking is whether your prayer at the Maiden's Ring healed your mother — may she always keep well!" she added, making a lucky sign. "Or whether it was the Irish monk, Columba, a dove according to his name, but a warrior in other ways, from all that I hear."

"A great lord too," said Bel, "yet he doesn't have any slaves. He walks about barefoot. He carries little babies and gives thralls a kiss of love."

"Very strange indeed!" Winnag agreed.

"The priests in the temple don't do that," Bel went on. "We were at the Maiden's Ring for the Solstice, Winnag. They celebrate the summer and the light, but they never speak to the people. They're far above us, set apart and holy and when they pray or sacrifice for us they make sure we pay them well. . . ." she paused, remembering her mother's armband.

Winnag nodded. "Long, long ago in the days when Earth Mother mourned the death of Corn Maiden, her bright young darling, there was neither temple nor priest, but a Wise Woman prayed for the people in a hut woven of willow . . ." she began, but Bel's mind was on the present and she didn't pay any attention.

"Just the same, the priest, Wyn, wouldn't take my scone," she mused, half to herself. "He said I was a Gifted One, whatever that means, favoured and chosen . . . Why, what's the matter?" she asked in alarm, for Winnag was trying to drag her creaking bones up from the ground.

"Well now, Bel, chosen and favoured — that's a terrible thing. I knew it, though, when you came to my hut with your questions. Only seekers after truth dare defy their gods and their kinsfolk. Searching is hard, but seekers sometimes find. Chosen and favoured and gifted, they say. Oh, child, be careful!"

"What do you mean?" asked Bel. "Are you frightened of me, Winnag?"

"No, dearie," the old woman said, more calmly, "not frightened *of* you, but *for* you a little, perhaps. Indeed, I'm honoured to have you in my poor hut. Bel, my dear, help me to my feet and we'll go outside into the sun for a moment."

So Bel helped old Winnag totter outside her ramshackle hut.

It was another hot day in a rare summer of almost endless sunshine which was already filled with trouble. Cattle were dying in the glen and milk was no longer safe to drink. Old people, whose rattling chests had survived the winter, gasped in the heat and gave up their struggle, paying the price of the sun which set wild flowers springing over the moorland, poured juice into berries and ripened the corn.

Around Winnag's hut the earth was dotted with yellow camomile and flavoured with the smell of wild garlic and thyme.

"Pick a handful of grass and wild flowers, dearie," said Winnag. "Take off your sandals. Let your young feet be naked like mine."

Bel obeyed.

"Now give me the flowers and pick up a handful of earth as well," Winnag said. Bel dug with her fingers and her nails filled with dirt.

"Hold out your hands now," said Winnag, and she spread the earth over one of Bel's outstretched palms and scattered the warm pungent grasses, already withering, over the other.

"Oh, Bel," she said, and there were tears in her eyes, "you should be garlanded with flowers and attended by maidens, our Midsummer Lady clad in garments of green. But there's only old Winnag to pay you poor homage. Now, listen, lassie, I've put into your two hands the earth and its fruits. To win them is hard toil indeed, yet it's the very same earth which gives us our dignity, our rights and inheritance. For all men: kings, warriors, poets, priests, peasants and thralls, and each of us women, however ill-regarded, have our place and our belonging in this earth. The brown earth beneath us nurses us and feeds us. The green hills about us guard us, enfold us, and this is our birthright. Therefore, Bel of the heart-searchings, lass of the questings, never forget to love this dear earth!"

Bel nodded, "Oh, I do love it, Winnag!" she said. "I love our glen, the hill where deer run, the rowans and hazels, and the burn too. Columba poured water over the baby and the thralls he marked with the cross. And there's the sea too. You were going to tell me a story about it, remember?"

"I was indeed, lassie, and I shall. I hadn't forgotten the water either, for is it not part of the same good three? The earth and her fruits need the swift flowing water . . ."

"Not so swift flowing these days," said Bel, dropping the earth and the grasses and brushing her damp palms together. "There's been no rain at all and the water is low. I'm worried in case there's another drought," she added, putting on her sandals again.

Winnag didn't answer, but she shot Bel a glance from her far-seeing, watery eyes. Then she tottered back into her hut.

"You know, Winnag, I'm still thinking about those priests in the temple," Bel said, and this time it was she who poured out a drink for them both, not primroses, but camomile. "As

44

I said, they don't bother with ordinary people like Columba does. They wear rich clothes and soft shoes, and you should have smelt their good dinner!'

Winnag nodded. "They have the power, dearie. They took it from our Wise Woman long ago when bright warriors of your mother's race invaded our glen with swords of sharp iron. The only iron my people ever had was the thrall's collar," she added sadly. "Yes, the priests took the power, but, as you say so rightly, they lost touch with the people. Your Columba sounds a good man," she added.

"It costs him a lot," Bel tried to explain. "He said so himself, and besides, I could see it. He's thrown away all the usual weapons men fight with."

"Has he now?"

"Yes, and Coll — that's the slave boy I met, says he wins battles without needing to use weapons. Have you ever heard of such a thing?"

"I have not," Winnag agreed. "Not among men," she added, but Bel rushed on.

"But I think I know what Coll means, because when I got home my mother was better, as I told you. Oh, what do you think, Winnag? Was it Columba, or . . . ?"

Winnag stared into the camomile brew in her beaker. "A good word spoken in blessing is worth a lot," she murmured. "Lass, let's just be glad that your mother is well."

But Bel shook her head, for it wasn't enough. She felt she had to know more.

"Come now, Midsummer Lady," Winnag cajoled her, "I'll tell you my story, shall I?"

"Yes, please, Winnag," Bel said.

"Well now," said Winnag, "you wnted to know why burn water is sweet when the sea is so salty you would die if you drank it. Then you must know that once upon a time two sisters lived in an ancient stronghold beside the sea. Only the sea wasn't salty then, and neither did it move in and out, mourning and lamenting, as it does now. It was as still as water is when winter lays cold hands upon it, and it shimmered like a piece of fairy cloth, beautiful to the eye, as well as tasting very sweet. So every day the two sisters, who were called Sel and Sula, went there for water. At least Sula did, while Sel drank from silver goblets the water her sister fetched.

"Now I should tell you that the two sisters lived together in great happiness, with never a sharp word between them, and never a salt tear shed. And they lived like this because Sula did everything Sel wanted, fetching and carrying, not only water but everything else they needed as well, while her sister sat with her two white hands, each as soft as fairy cloth, folded on her lap. But if her hands were still her lips were busy, for Sel was a singer. From her mouth came such music that people hurried from all over the wide world to hear it, and in that music was healing and peace.

"And that is why Sula waited on Sel and fetched and carried for her and said never a sharp word to her nor shed a salt tear. Her sister's singing sweetened her days and made every burden light.

"One day Sel asked Sula, shaping her request into music so lovely that the skylarks stopped singing to listen, 'Sister mine, over the hillside, beyond the brae* grow purple brambles sweeter than anything I have ever tasted. Gather me some. My singing will help you, and lighten your way.'

"So Sula took a basket and went to gather brambles. She walked easily, with a light step because, as Sel promised, her sister sat with folded hands and sang.

"But the hillside was very far away, further than Sula had ever been, and when she reached it, she found it steep and rocky. Worse still, Sel's music no longer reached her ears. Still, she carried on, but the way was hard without her sister's music and soon her feet were cut and bleeding. The brambles tore her hands and hurt her so much that tears flowed down her cheeks. She tasted salt on her lips. Sorrow has always a bitter taste.

"All stained with bramble juice and blood Sula made her weary way home, straining her ears to hear Sel's singing, but never a sound came to her, and when she got home everything was as still as the shimmering water outside their stronghold. Very anxiously Sula hurried in, and found her sister curled up asleep beside the fire, which she hadn't thought of feeding, so it had gone out, a thing unheard of then and now.

"Sula was so tired and weary that she shook Sel

* brae = hillside

awake, staining her sister's snowy shoulders with the juice and blood on her hands, and speaking harshly to her, with words and a tone of voice neither sister had ever heard.

"And Sel, startled at seeing her sister in such a state, reproached herself bitterly, so bitterly indeed that she began to cry. In her grief she rushed down to the sea and threw herself into the water.

"Now the sea, you will recall, was saltless and still, but Sel's grief was such that her salt tears flowed without ceasing into the sea. Sula had followed her sister to the shore. She started to cry too, filled with remorse at the harsh words she had spoken. Then she flung herself into the sea after her sister.

"But now a change came over the sweet, still water. Filled with so many tears it became salt. As Sula stretched out her arms, struggling to embrace her sister, the calm surface of the sea was broken. Waves began to swell and fall.

"From that day to this the two sisters search for one another under the sea, shedding salt tears while the waves above them rock and sigh.

"That's nearly the end of the story, but I must tell you that Sel grew a long fish tail. She became a mermaid and still today when the winds rise and the waves grow high you may hear Sel's lovely voice singing her wild laments for her sister.

"Sula however could never forget the shore where she always used to go for her water, or the far hillsides where purple brambles grow, and, besides, she had carried the brambles at such cost so far and never tasted any. She grew a furry coat to keep her warm in the salt water, but sometimes she leaves the waves and lies on the shore, looking about her with mournful eyes!'

"She'd become a seal!" exclaimed Bel.

"Yes," said Winnag. "It's said of seals that there are times when they shed their coats and wander in human form over the shore to the far hill, and then we know that Sula is searching for brambles, longing to taste what she went so far to find, longing for the stronghold and the fire as well; and the thing which draws her is music. She listens to music, thinking it is her lost sister's singing, and replies to it too with a sad drawn-out wail."

"Poor Sula," said Bel, "and poor Sel too. I've never seen a mermaid or heard one sing, but I've certainly heard the seals. I'll think of your story, Winnag, next time I'm at the sea and taste the salt water and see the seals with their sad eyes. But you still haven't told me why burn water is sweet."

"You're the persistent one with your questions!" said Winnag, and Bel thought, "That's what Wyn said. Only his voice was angry. I won't tell Winnag, though. I don't want her to get worried. And I don't want her to look at me in that frightened way again, almost as though she wanted to bow down to me. I'm not special. I'm just Bel."

But she felt a shiver inside her, and so she said,

extra brightly, "It was a good story, though, especially for someone who doesn't like the sea."

And now Winnag laughed, a thing Bel hadn't yet seen her do.

"Ah yes, but the sea is a thing of very great wonder," she said, "only, as I told you, it brought death to my people and we were, in any case, a people of the glen, the river and the hill, though we've vanished now without trace. No one speaks our language now. Echoes of it linger in the old names, especially of rivers. Through force or cunning, magic or marriage and even, sometimes, it may be love, we've mingled our blood with the blood of your people, our conqueror, and blood has its own way of speaking, you know."

"I'm not sure if I understand you, Winnag," said Bel, "but I'm sorry that it was my mother's people who brought death to yours."

"Oh, but it was long ago," smiled Winnag, "a thousand years, or so."

"Yet there's a saying that the Dark People will never disappear from our glen," said Bel.

"Likely enough — and that makes me happy."

"What about fairies?' asked Bel. "Is it true that they are your people too?"

"That's likely enough as well, but how and why is another story," said Winnag.

"Tell me," begged Bel, but Winnag shook her head. "Not today, dearie," she said. "We've done enough for today. Why, you've stood with naked feet on the naked earth and been the Midsummer Lady. We've had a celebration with a story to tell and camomile to drink. I'm tired now, Bel. We'll tell that other story all in good time."

And Bel had to agree. She thanked Winnag for the celebration, as the old woman had called it, and set off home, clambering up the hill. She wondered if Winnag knew many more stories. It was a pity mothers wouldn't allow their children near her to hear them. That evening Bel told her little sisters, Elir, Genann and Mooreen, the story of Sel and Sula whose salt tears filled the sea. She looked forward to visiting Winnag again and hearing another story, but many months were to pass before she met the old woman. Just the same, Winnag of the Dark People had become part of Bel's own story; though the old woman would have said it was just Earth Mother and Corn Maiden intertwining old tales to make life go on in the glen.

5

CHOSEN TO DIE

That summer there was hardly any rain. People began to wait and listen for it, but day after day went by and no rain fell, until . . .

"Listen!" Bel said to her sisters late one evening. "There's the rain!"

"At last!" they exclaimed and they all rushed out to see. Their mother put an old pot under the thatch of their roof. "With luck there will be some water in there by morning," she said, and, sure enough, there was.

It rained for four days, almost without stopping, and the burn chuckled as it raced over the stones. But then the rain went off and no more fell for a long time, until the barley was almost ready to be harvested. Heavy showers flattened the crops, but then the sun shone again.

"I've never known a summer like this," Bel's father said, sweating under the load he carried. "It's good in some ways, but bad in others. There's a feverish sickness spreading through the High Fort. A child died today."

The sickness spread all through the glen. Bel had a headache. The little girls weren't well.

Genann was the worst. She lay in a fever and ate no food for a week, no matter how her mother and Bel tried to coax her.

The red deer on the hill came close to the homestead in search of green things to eat. Bel saw them each evening as she scraped low trickles of water into her leather bottles at the burn.

There was no sign of Columba, but his monks were to be seen all over the hillsides, gathering herbs and making medicines which they took with their prayers to the sick people in the glen.

"They're good, holy men," said Bel's father, "and some, like Columba himself, belong to the royal blood of Ireland, yet they nurse sick folk and never turn anyone away from the small round huts they've made themselves. They chant their hymns and psalms and pray. King Connail in the High Fort follows their Christ, and so did my own folk when I was small. I think we should too."

But Bel's mother touched the lucky bone she wore round her neck. "There are all kinds of powers," she said. "if we turn from our old gods they will come and attack us. With the drought and all this sickness we'd better not risk bringing their anger on us. Is Derril not back from his fishing?"

"Not yet," said her husband, "but the river's so low, I doubt he'll catch much."

He was right. Derril came with such a small fish that they gave it to the cat.

Genann got better, but remained weak and couldn't be bothered with anything. Bel wondered if she should visit Winnag to see if she had any advice to offer, but there were berries to be collected and crushed into juice and she was kept too busy.

"The rowans are red now," said her mother. "But still there's no rain."

She went outside. They heard her scream and ran out to see what the matter was.

"Look," she pointed. Three crows rose from the forest and flapped with slow steady wing beats over the homestead. They were very black against the evening sky.

"Not one, but three," she whispered. "There's death in that seeing."

The family watched the crows, bringers of evil, fly over their rooftop and across the glen in the direction of the Maiden's Ring.

"Where is Columba?" thought Bel, suddenly sensing a way out of ill-luck and terror. Columba would be sure to challenge the power of the dark. He would fight against it with stronger weapons than any sword, though what those weapons were, Bel wasn't sure. His prayers, she supposed, and the name of his God.

But no one knew where Columba was. Perhaps he had gone back to the green island in the west where he lived among white sands, seals and the endless sound of the sea.

"We need him here," Bel thought. "But what about our own priests then? Haven't they any power against sickness and death in the glen?'

She didn't dare voice this thought to anyone.

"I'll go and ask Winnag," she decided. "I'll go tomorrow. It's getting dark now."

The long light evenings were coming to an end, but it was still very warm and the air was still. You could walk out in the evenings without any warm covering, and still no rain fell.

Bel decided to go out anyway and get some air. Perhaps she would see the deer, though she hoped they wouldn't be plagued with flies as they so often were, these stuffy warm evenings.

Not flies, but midges! They bit Bel before she saw them. She stood under the rowans, rubbing her bare arms, her wrists, ankles, legs, face, bitten all over by swarms of tiny insects. "This is useless," she thought, and was about to go in when dogs barking on the other side of the burn warned her of the coming of strangers. She stared westwards against the darkening moorland and saw a procession move with much ceremony across the glen.

"They've come from the temple" she thought with a shiver of fear. "What can they be doing?"

Her mother came out and looked across the glen.

"Priests from the temple," said Bel, pointing.

"Coming here at nightfall!" exclaimed her mother, and called to her husband. The little girls came outside and stared at the strangers, though they clung close to their mother. Derril stood beside his father, fondling the young puppy his uncle had just given him. Bel stayed where she was under the trees.

In the fading light a bat fluttered past them and an owl hooted from over the hill.

"Bat-time, owl-time!" Bel's mother trembled. "What do *they* want? Why are they coming here?"

Sensing her mother's terror, Genann started to cry, and still Bel stood alone under the rowans, almost as if she knew . . . as if she had always known, from that day in the temple, when Wyn hailed her as chosen, gifted and favoured; or, no, perhaps even before that, when questions had stirred in her, questions about the sweet-tasting water, about why death destroys deer and babies, even before they are properly born. She had known all summer when the glen seemed to sicken, that there would be a price to pay, and now fear rose up inside her, keeping her rooted to the spot.

It didn't surprise her at all that the priest at the very head of the procession was Wyn.

He bowed deeply to Bel's parents. "We honour you because the gods have chosen your daughter," he said, and slaves spread lavish gifts at the feet of Bel's frightened family: wine, honey, amber, sacks bulging with sweet-smelling herbs, oils, a box of clucking chickens, a goat on a rope and bales of finely woven cloth.

Bel's parents looked at one another. Bel could guess her father's dismay and her mother's desire to fill her carved kist with undreamt of luxuries. She knew her father wouldn't dare, and her mother wouldn't dream of refusing the priest's bounty.

She looked for Coll among the slaves. He was nowhere to be seen. She could only hope he was safe and well.

Her father found his voice. "Lords, my family and I are poor but there's a place at our fire and you are welcome."

Wyn thanked him. They hadn't come expecting hospitality, he explained, but instead to do the family a very great honour, and now for the first time he looked across at Bel.

"The gods have chosen your daughter to be offered as a sacrifice at the Ring,' he said.

Bel's mother choked back a scream. Her father dropped his hands and looked over at Bel. And now they were all looking at her. She felt their stares bite more cruelly than midges. She glanced up the hill behind her but there was no escape for her there.

"Need and sickness have arisen. It's time to turn back to the gods and honour the old ways," Wyn said.

"We *have* honoured the old ways," thought Bel. "We've prayed in the temple and my mother gave you her armband, but sickness and drought and death still came to our glen."

"Sir, she's only a child," Bel's mother began.

"The gods need a girl," said Wyn, "someone older than a mere child, but not yet a woman, to be offered at Samhain Feast when the dark of the year begins."

And now Bel started to cry. The little girls cried too. She could hear them, but she couldn't

57

stop them or herself.

"No!" she sobbed. "No!"

Strong hands laid hold of her.

"Help me!" she sobbed, but her mother was screaming too and her father was shaking helplessly. Neither of them could do anything to save her.

Columba might have helped her, but he was far away on his lonely green island. Winnag? But the smelly old woman who had crowned her Midsummer Lady had no charms against the power of the priests. Nothing could help Bel as tall slaves dragged her, screaming, to Wyn.

His annoyed eyes frowned beneath his crown of owl feathers. "Silly one!" he scolded. "You'll wear a crown of rubies redder than rowans and taste the finest food you've ever eaten! You'll be pampered and petted like a royal princess and hear long poems in your honour."

He went on and on. Bel stared at him in disbelief. What did she want with a crown of rubies or poems or fine food when they were going to kill her? Sobs tore her apart. She shuddered. The last light was leaving the sky. All around her torches flared.

"Why take her now?" she heard her father plead. "Our corn's still not gathered. The leaves on the trees are hardly turning to yellow. It's a long time yet till Samhain Feast!"

"The sacrifice must be made ready," Wyn answered coldly, and Bel stared at him through her tears. Sacrifice! That was it, the word she had

58

dreaded. Did Winnag know something about it? Had she made some sort of magic against Bel when she had told her to stand barefoot on the earth after she had heard that Bel had been called favoured and chosen?

Chosen to die.

Horror took hold of her, too strongly for screaming. She looked all about her but the torch-flares had blotted out both the hill and the homestead. High above were small pinpricks of stars, too far away for hope or help. Numbly she let slaves load her on a long wagon drawn by two oxen which twitched their ears in the emptiness of the night.

Bel had never been out so late before. The cart lurched on, surrounded by men carrying torches, and Bel looked about her, rubbing her midge bites, hardly able to believe that this dark world was her own glen.

Out of the darkness came the eerie cry of owls. Bel pitied small furry things, scurrying helplessly to hide.

"As helpless as me," she thought, starting to cry again as the wagon jolted on towards the temple.

She heard the sound of the river. Soon they would reach the spot where she had seen Columba. He had blessed her and her family, and his words had driven death away from her mother. But now death had come to attack them again.

"Only it's me this time," Bel thought, "and Columba is too far away to help."

But did that mean his blessing was far away too? Were the words of protection just for that one time only? Bel tried hard to remember what Columba had said. 'All within your house,' he had prayed, and those words, she believed, had made her mother well, but she recalled Columba had prayed three times "always".

That was it! "May God the Father always guard you, God the Son always protect you, and God the Spirit always bless you and all within your house."

Bel stopped crying. She looked up at the stars swirling overhead, watching her glen in its quiet sleep, just as they had always done.

"Shining stars," whispered Bel, "can you see me down here? Listen then. I take the guarding and protection and blessing of Columba's God."

She held up her hand as a sign that she meant what she said and into her mind came the song the barefoot monks had sung beside the river.

These are the Three Guarding Ones:
Father, Spirit and the Son.
Be ever with us, Lord, we pray,
each noon, each dark, each break of day.

Bel sang the song over again to herself. "Each noon, each dark, each break of day," she repeated the last line softly and now felt comforted, even though she was alone in the night, surrounded by people who planned to harm her.

"Night is good," she thought. "it covers the

glen like a blanket. How tired I am! I should like to lie and sleep too.''

Beneath a fountain of stars they led Bel, unprotesting, into the temple courtyard. Women surrounded her. The sea of unknown faces was frightening, but she was too tired to care. Besides, she still had the sense of being comforted and protected. She let them lead her into a firelit room and to a sweet-smelling mattress of hay and dried herbs which reminded her of Winnag and her Midsummer celebration. The mattress was covered with woven linen with blankets on top. Bel lay down on hay between flax and wool and fell asleep straight away. She was all alone and chosen to die, but a sense of comfort drove her fear away and her dreams were full of smiling stars.

6

CORN MAIDEN IS FRIGHTENED

Bel woke up next morning, bewildered at finding herself away from her own fireside, with strange sounds all about her.

"Where am I?" she thought. Then she remembered and fear, grief and homesickness took hold of her. Tears sprang to her eyes and a lump rose into her throat, but there was no one to hear or help her, except, she noticed suddenly, a woman, a slave who must have been ordered to guard her.

She stared around the wooden room in horror, but the woman, seeing that she was now awake, came across to her on soundless bare feet.

She spoke to Bel with her eyes carefully turned away, calling her "the Maiden", as though Bel wasn't really there at all.

"Is the Maiden rested? Will she come and eat?" she asked.

"I want to go home," said Bel, but the woman didn't answer. Instead she gave a signal and more women came in. They too kept their faces turned away. They brought Bel bread made from white flour, with a sweet comb of honey, fruit juice and meat, but Bel longed for the sour taste of barley bread, goat's milk and oatmeal at her own fireside. Surrounded by strangers, who wouldn't look at her, the fine food seemed tasteless and Bel hardly ate any.

The women pulled off her woollen dress and washed her in warm, scented water. No one except her mother had done this for her before, and Bel hated the hands of strangers on her. They gave her soft undergarments, then pulled on a long dress of fine woven cloth, brightly coloured in all the colours of the rainbow and stiff with embroidery. They loaded her neck, arms and fingers with jewels: golden chains, amethysts, pearls, beads of amber, coral and jet. They brushed her long red hair, braided it and wound it round her head and threaded more jewels through it. They showed her a piece of polished metal so that she could study her reflection, and Bel gasped in surprise. She wished her mother could have seen her, and her little sisters. That longing took the sparkle from her eyes and the colour from her face.

Besides, in a dress heavy with jewels and with her hair so carefully braided how could she run out into the wind or wet her feet in the burn?

She sat on a carved chair and priests came and bowed down to her, and, just as Wyn promised, a bard began to compose a long poem in her praise, but Bel felt lost, almost as though they had buried her alive inside her fine clothing. Her head ached. She wanted to go home. The jewels and rich dresses they brought her each day choked her like a slave's collar. She wondered if Coll had felt like this when strangers had put the heavy iron collar round his neck.

What good to her now were charms or prayers of protection? Day after day dragged by, and each one was dull and hopeless. Soon Bel stopped thinking, "I want to go home." There was just a huge ache inside her. "No one cares about me any more," she thought. "No one at all."

The ache was like a heavy stone. Bel didn't feel like eating. "All that good food is wasted on me. Give it to my family instead," she told the servants. But it was like talking to a wall. They kept their faces turned from her, and silently removed plates heaped high with uneaten food.

"Why doesn't father tell the king to send his warriors to rescue me?" Bel wondered, but she knew that would mean war in the glen. And she knew, and King Connail surely knew, that few even of his bravest warriors would defy the power of the priests.

"So I'm going to die," she thought.

Now every day seemed as heavy as the woven robes she wore, while at night she tossed and turned, unable to sleep, making the mattress under her lumpy and the bedding uncomfortable.

The priests must have felt concerned about her, for they brought Bel's family to see her, but that was worse, far worse. From the other side of the wooden enclosure, Elir, Genann and Mooreen stared at Bel, their thumbs in their mouths, almost as though she were dead

64

already. They started to cry and Bel burst into tears too.

"Take me home. Help me!" she begged, though she knew it was useless. Her mother began to cry too.

"I can't bear it, shut away here," sobbed Bel. "How much longer is it till Samhain Feast?"

Her father counted on his fingers. It was about six weeks, he reckoned.

Six weeks! It seemed an eternity, and yet, once it ended, Bel would be led out to die.

"I can't bear it!" she repeated. "Oh, why did all this have to happen to me?'

But there was no answer to that question either.

"I don't want to die!" Bel sobbed and her mother outside the enclosure cried even more helplessly, while her father, strong man though he was, one of the king's warriors, paced up and down, powerless to help.

"The king . . .' began Bel, but her father shook his head. The king's family had long since followed the Christian faith, but King Connail himself was powerless against the priests.

Bel cried even harder, and the priests had to send her family away.

Wyn himself came and spoke sternly to Bel, but nothing he said helped her.

"You'll make yourself ugly, and spoil your dress," he scolded.

"I don't care if I'm ugly," sobbed Bel. "I'd rather be ugly than dead!"

The tall priest shrugged helplessly and walked away, leaving her crying. There was nothing he, or anyone could do.

Her grief, rage and homesickness together with lack of food and sleep soon made Bel ill. Charms were said, tempting meals provided, dead moles were festooned above her bed (a sure cure for weakness), but nothing made Bel any better, and in the end the priests, afraid that she would die before Samhain Feast, did the only thing they could think of. They sent for Winnag of the Dark Ones with her charms and lore.

Day after day Winnag sat beside Bel and moistened her forehead with fresh water. She crooned old songs to coax her back to life and strength.

"Earth Mother loved her darling Corn Maiden, the child of Spring Queen and the golden Harvest Lord," Winnag began.

" 'Dance, dance, Corn Maiden! Leap with your green dress into the world.'

"But Corn Maiden lay sleeping in her dark chamber and didn't want to leap up into the cold windy world.

"Earth Mother whispered to the Sky Sisters: 'Weep for Corn Maiden who lies lost to the world.'

"So the Sky Sisters shed their soft tears in abundance. Corn Maiden heard them lamenting, stirred in the sleep, and Earth Mother heard.

" 'Dance, kingly Sun and lead Corn Maiden up into the world.'

"So the kingly Sun stepped out in a royal dance, and Corn Maiden smiled as his warm hand touched hers.

" 'Sky Sisters and Sunshine, knock at Corn Maiden's window and tell her the fields are empty. She must get up now and dance though the world,' ordered Earth Mother.

" 'Who's there? Who is it calling? Who wants me?' asks sleepy Corn Maiden.

" 'I'm the sun,' smiled His Majesty, in as royal a voice as you've ever heard. 'Warm fields are waiting. Come on, Corn Maiden. Dance in the world.'

" 'Please heed us,' pleaded the Sky Spirits, weeping. 'We need you, Corn Maiden. Put on your green dress and come back to the world.'

"So Corn Maiden put on her green dress and held out her hands. The sun and the rain took them and led her up into the world. They bowed and they curtsied and danced hand-in-hand over fields and hillsides.

"But summer yellowed Corn Maiden's garments and dyed her hair gold. Then Earth Mother knew that sharp knives would soon cut Corn Maiden to the ground. . . ."

"Don't," said Bel, sharply, the first word she had spoken for days.

"We must," answered Winnag. "Be Corn Maiden now, Bel, and we'll finish the story together."

"I don't want to die," said Bel. "Corn Maiden is frightened. The knives are sharp and Earth

Mother should know how sweet and dear life is in the glen . . .'

"But listen, Bel, it's only by the death of Corn Maiden that life can go on in the glen."

"I don't care," said Bel crossly. "I'm not Corn Maiden and I don't want to die. Go away, Winnag, you can't help me either."

"No?" queried Winnag, "Well, here's another story."

Bel shifted impatiently, tired of the old woman and her tales.

"Once there was an old woman who had nothing in the world but one little red-brown calf. Such a dear creature! But cruel men with great power came and stole her one little calf. The old woman ran up and down the glen with loud lamenting. She had no one to turn to, and in the end she threw herself on to the kindly earth, where all our sorrows must end one day, my dearie. She slept, as only those stricken with grief sleep, and when she woke it was to the sound of a man's voice singing. The old woman had heard many a singer and many a song, but never a singer like that, had she heard, nor ever a song."

"Go on," said Bel.

"The singer had a voice of great power, but his head and his hands held up to the wide skies and his feet in the bracken were all bare. And his song was a prayer."

"Columba!" exclaimed Bel. "But he's away in the west!"

"To a green, holy island which is too small to hold for long a man like Columba, a king-maker and king-breaker, I'm told, who is proud and hot-tempered among the haughty, but humble to the humble, and kind, oh, my dear, how kind to the poor!"

Bel held her breath and Winnag went on with her tale. "When the prayer and the song were finished the old woman drew near him and told him her trouble. 'Go home and be happy,' answered Columba. 'As your faith is, so shall the end of your trouble be.'

"And now the old woman trembled. 'Sir, I have no faith,' she said, 'but the little lost calf, that dearest small creature you yourself have held beneath the hollow of your hand and blessed with good words of protection.' "

Bel stared at the old woman, "Winnag, I think I know what your story means. The old woman's yourself, isn't she? Did you really meet Columba?"

"I did indeed and no sooner did I get back home from meeting him than certain powerful ones from the temple sent word for me to come here. There are times, do you see, when they need my old ways and wisdom. So I came, but I can see that my news of Columba and not my herbs has restored the sparkle to your eyes," she finished with a smile.

Bel smiled back. "Your story helped too, but I can tell you one thing. I've never been called a calf before!"

"Now, see," said Winnag, still smiling, "there's always a first time."

Bel nodded, hardly able to take in Winnag's story. It amazed her that the old woman cared so much for her. She began to feel ashamed that she had ever suspected that Winnag might have brought trouble on her. She felt ashamed too that in her fears and grief she had forgotten those words: "May God guard you always, each noon, each dark, each break of day."

"What did Columba say when you reminded him of his blessing?" she asked Winnag.

"He said: 'May the Spirit of wisdom give you the faith you need. Go home and you shall find the little lost creature you love.' And see, I have," finished Winnag.

"He didn't say . . ." Bel hesitated, "anything more about me? That he would come and rescue me?"

"It will be as our faith is," Winnag reminded her. "What more can we do? I'm a woman of the glen. I don't know these new ways. But listen, dearie, on my way here I met a boy with a thrall's collar round his neck. He gave me this for you." She searched among the layers of rags which covered her bony old body and produced two twigs tied together in a cross.

"He said you would know what this sign meant — and, as you can see, it's been cut from the rowan."

"It's from Coll, then! It must be! Yes, I know what it means, Winnag. It's the sign Columba

70

made with his thumb on the baby's forehead. He made it over me too when he blessed me. He said, 'May God the Father always guard you, God the Son always protect you, and God the Spirit always bless you, and all within your house.' Coll must have heard those words. He has sent me this cross to remind me about them. He made it out of rowan because he cut me a rowan blossom when we first met. Oh, Winnag, I am lucky. I was so unhappy but now two good friends have found me — and Columba knows about me too. How is Coll?"

"He seemed well enough," said Winnag, "and you are looking so much better. You must eat now."

Bel pulled a face. "Must I? I hate the food here, Winnag. I want to go home. But I feel better after all that you've told me." She looked down at the wooden cross. "I prayed Columba's prayer the first night, but afterwards I forgot. Oh, I wish I could speak to Coll!"

"That should be easy enough," Winnag said. "You are the Favoured One, the Maiden of old destiny. So long as you don't ask to go home the priests should give you anything else you want."

Bel's face cleared. "Not dresses or jewellery, though it was all very beautiful, nor waiting women who never look at me, or poems of praise either," she said. "Tel Wyn I want you and Coll to look after me, if anyone must. I want you and Coll to be with me every day. I'd like to go outside too and feel the wind in my hair again. And I'd like to see my family properly, not separated by a high fence. I'd like them to know . . . about Columba," she explained, dropping her voice again.

"You're wise to speak quietly. In fact, better not to name that name, except in hidden ways," said Winnag. "Eat some food then, Bel, and I shall find Wyn and tell him you have come back from the shadowlands and now he must give you whatever you want. Winnag of the Glen and Coll of the Iron Collar shall attend you, my dear, though the Great Ones will think we're odd companions for someone as special as you."

"Let them think what they want," said Bel. "You're my friends and it's good to have you here. Whatever lies ahead, I know I'm not alone."

"That's good," said Winnag, and repeated, "Winnag of the Glen and Coll of the Iron Collar," but this time she added, "and Columba of the Guarding Love. I am an old woman, Bel, and, as you know, my people were conquered by iron swords. I do not hold to the power of either warriors or priests, but I have named three people who hold about you a power which is stronger than Wyn can ever guess: the love of our hearts, as well as the guarding of the Christ of Columba the meek. Hold to that, dearie, through good and through ill."

"I shall," promised Bel and, as Winnag shuffled away on her thin legs, Bel raised Coll's cross up towards the light and prayed Columba's prayer, only this time she changed the words to make it a special prayer for her:

May God the Father always guard me,
And God the Son always protect me,
And God the Spirit always bless me
and all within my house.

Then she ate a large piece of white bread and honey, and enjoyed every bite of it. And she looked forward to seeing Coll again.

7

"MY DEFENCE IS
MY CHRIST"

The next person to appear was Coll. He came in nervously, but Bel welcomed him warmly. "Thank you for your cross, Coll," she said from her high carved chair.

His face cleared. He came and stood beside her. "You still remember me?" he asked.

"Coll, I've never forgotten you! How could I? Did Wyn beat you?"

"His slaves did. They beat me often now. It's terrible. I wanted to run away but there's nowhere to go."

"I'm sorry," said Bel.

"It's all right," Coll went on. "Eochdair, one of Columba's monks, helps me. I meet him at the Ring or else we go to his little hut and we talk. He brings me bread sometimes. And he explains the holy Scriptures to me. But what about you, Bel? I was so sad when I heard it was you they'd chosen."

"They're going to kill me," said Bel, and her eyes filled with tears. "They made me wear fine dresses and load of jewellery. It was gorgeous, but it choked me. I felt like you must have done when they put the iron collar on you. Was that bad, Coll?''

Coll nodded. "It still is." He dropped his voice. "I told Eochdair about you," he said.

"And Winnag has met Columba. But, oh Coll, what can they do against the priests? I don't think anyone can help me now."

"Don't say that, Bel. The priests are very strong; I know that only too well. But their gods are shadowy and dark. Eochdair says so, and I'm sure he is right. That's why I sent you that cross."

"Winnag says it's made of rowan. I gave you rowan blossom for luck, remember?"

"Of course I do," said Coll.

"Did you make the shape of a cross because of Columba?" asked Bel. "Sit down and tell me."

Coll smiled. "I think it would be better if I stay standing. It's amazing that they've allowed us this much. No one is supposed to speak to the Maiden, you know."

"Yes, I know that only too well! That was horrible too. Now, we were talking about your cross. It's the shape Columba made when he poured water over you. He made it over me too when he prayed for protection. What does it mean exactly, Coll?'

"Columba made that shape because Christ, who is High King of Heaven, came to this world and died on a cross . . ." Coll explained.

Bel looked down at the cross Coll had made. "But I'm going to have to die, Coll."

75

"I know," Coll said, "Unless . . ."

"Unless?"

"Unless something happens. I shall pray for you, Bel."

"Will you? For me? Oh, Coll, you'd better pray hard! As soon as the moon appears at Samhain Feast they'll take me to the Ring and kill me."

He nodded, "Oh, Bel, to think you gave me rowans for luck! But prayer is stronger than luck. And you know, it was after meeting you that time that I first met Columba."

"Tell me about that too," said Bel.

So Coll told his story standing beside Bel with the iron collar round his neck and his eyes bright with a new hope.

He had set off towards the priests' enclosure, still with Bel's blossom pinned to him, and on his way had met Columba and his monks walking through the glen.

"I didn't dare go up to him and speak to him, but he seemed to know that I wanted to, just the same."

"Just as he seemed to know about my problems by the river that time."

"It's because of his prayers," Coll explained. "It gives him an understanding about people. He could be rich and powerful, but he has made himself just like a slave — remember he said so. I think that gives him power too, because if you truly want only the honour of your master then you don't feel that what happens to you is so important."

"I think I know what you mean," said Bel. "Go on. Did he speak to you, then?"

"He said, 'You're wearing a slave's collar and your feet are bent to your master's bidding but you will be bound by the love of the King of Kings and walk where he leads'," Coll quoted. "And then he began to pray and something far bigger than me took hold of me. I knew it was more real and important and more powerful too than Wyn."

Bel nodded, "Winnag thinks so too, and so do I whenever I pray Columba's prayer. It makes me happy and strong. I felt that way when I first came here, but then I forgot all about the prayer. Until Winnag brought me your cross and told me she had met Columba. Then I began to feel that there might be some hope for me."

"I'm sure there's hope for you, Bel," Coll told her warmly.

"It can't be long till Samhain Feast," Bel reminded him.

"Three weeks, I think," Col told her.

"Three weeks!" she shivered. "It's hard having to wait, and yet, I don't want the time to go quickly either. Look at the sunshine, Coll! It's so long since I felt the sun or the wind. Do you think I could go outside, right outside, I mean, not just in the yard? Winnag says the priests won't refuse anything, so long as I don't run away. Besides, where could I run to? If I went home it would only mean trouble for my family. I'd love to see them again, though, so long as we don't all cry!"

"Perhaps I could bring them here," said Coll. "I'm sure you could go outside, Bel, but you must take your cloak. It's much colder now than it was when you first came here."

So Bel pulled on a long woollen cloak. Coll had only a coarse tunic, but he said he didn't mind.

It was good to walk outside the yard into the wind and sun. Coll was right, it was much colder. The weather had changed, he explained, soon after Bel had been taken to the temple, and the rain had come.

"People said it was because the priests had chosen a Maiden," said Coll, "but they didn't say it too loudly because the king doesn't approve. And when the holy monks bring them medicines and gather them together to hear the Scriptures they don't say it at all. In fact many of them have been baptized as I was that time."

"Baptized? Was that when Columba poured water over you? Why did he do it?"

"It's a sign that we belong to Christ," explained Coll.

"I should like Columba to pour water over me one day," said Bel. "Oh, Coll, it's good to be outside. I'd almost forgotten what everything looks like," she added, as they crossed the moorland. Small black calves half-disappeared under their mothers' patient flanks.

"Look at those calves!" Bel said, almost as though she had never seen cows before. "I wonder if they know about Samhain? My mother says Wyn and the other priests believe that people go

78

on living after they die in islands beyond the West. Just think, Coll, beyond the sunset. It must be beautiful there. No one grows old. There's endless feasting, but it's only for warriors, not someone like me.

"Or me," Coll answered. "I'm only a slave. But I'm not just Wyn's slave now. I belong to Christ and there will be a place in his heaven for me. For us both," he added firmly.

"Even if I have to die?" wondered Bel aloud.

"Of course. But you mustn't think about dying. Columba says Jesus has died for the life of the world. So there's no need for you to die too."

"Are you sure?" asked Bel.

"Of course I'm sure," answered Coll. "Do you remember your prayer, Bel? The blessing Columba gave you and the song the monks sang?"

"The Three Guarding Ones?" asked Bel. "Of course I remember. Let's say that prayer together, Coll, and then we'd better go back before anyone comes looking for us.

So they held Bel's cross high and said the prayer the monks had chanted with voices which rose and fell like the tide:

These are the Three Guarding Ones,
Father, Spirit and the Son.
Be ever with us, Lord, we pray:
each noon, each dark, each break of day.

"That was good, Coll, and it's been good to talk to you."

"You're helping me too," said Coll, "and Wyn has told his slaves not to beat me because I'm guarding the Maiden."

"I'm glad," said Bel.

"I'll go and visit your family," promised Coll, "and tell them you'd like them to come and see you."

But Bel's family didn't come until the day of Samhain Feast, Bel's last day alive on earth. Just when there was so much everyone wanted to say, no one could think of anything. Once again Elir, Genann and Mooreen just stared at Bel. Sobs rose in Bel's throat, but she had already cried so much that she had no tears left.

"Tonight is Samhain Feast," she said in the strained silence between them. "The dead come close."

A gust of wind rustled through the trees. "Perhaps it's the dead whispering in dry thin voices," thought Bel, and she shivered, but then she looked at her family and tried to smile.

"Columba is very powerful." Her father said, trying to sound hopeful. "All over the glen people are following him. King Connail has become much braver since Columba came back to the High Fort from his island. I'm sure he came in time for Samhain Feast, Bel."

Bel nodded. "Coll and Winnag think so too," she said, "and you mustn't think badly of Winnag any more. She's been looking after me. She tells me stories. She knows lots of stories." She swallowed hard. "Whatever happens to me tonight I want you to look after Winnag,'' she managed to say, and her mother began to cry.

"Oh, Bel, what has brought all this trouble on you?'' she asked.

"It's because I asked those questions,'' explained Bel. "Wyn told me that a girl who thinks about things the way I do is sure to be highly favoured by the gods. Winnag says that's nonsense. She says I think about things because it's in my blood, but Coll says . . .'

"Well, you always were a gifted one in a way,'' her mother began, "but sometimes it's unwise to think too much, Bel.''

"I can't help being what I am,'' said Bel. "Where's Derril?''

"He's away with the other boys of his age at the High Fort, but he's very worried about you, Bel,'' said her father. "He wanted to come here and fight the priests and rescue you, but the other boys believe you can't fight against the gods. They will only bring misfortune on us.''

"That's right'', said Bel. "You can't fight them with swords, but Col is praying for me.''

"My own family used to believe in Christ,'' said Bel's father, "and when I see how brave you are, Bel, I think we've been wrong to forget that good faith and pray to the old gods of the glen.''

"I hate them!' said Bel's mother fiercely, but not too loudly. She touched her lucky bone. "Oh, Bel, how I miss you and all your songs and rhymes. I miss your help too . . .''

"I miss you,'' Bel began. She struggled with her

tears, but sorrow overcame her and she turned and fled out of the enclosure. Blinded by tears, she soon tripped and fell headlong.

In an instant there were bare feet in the grass beside her, strong hands about her and a voice in her ears, "Now, now, what's this, so full of haste and fear?" She was picked up and dusted down.

Bel looked up. "Oh!" she exclaimed and threw her arms around Columba. "I couldn't help it," she sobbed. "I've tried so hard. It was seeing my family again . . . I'm not afraid any more, really I'm not, but I'm only ten, and . . . oh, sir, are you going to be able to help me?"

A monk beside Columba was talking too, adding his explanations. Bel caught the words, "Coll, sacrifice, Samhain . . ."

"Go back to the enclosure, my child," said Columba, gently. "I have come here for this very reason, to tell the priests that these old cruel ways have no place now in Dalriada. White swan of my heart, be comforted. There's no wound too deep for the healing power of Christ the Lord, not even the black wound of death nor yet the red wound of sorrow, nor the white wound of fear." He laid his hand on Bel's shoulder and made the sign of the cross over her. She felt a throbbing beneath Columba's fingers. Peace replaced the fear in her heart and joy took the place of tears as she walked back towards the enclosure and the hue and cry which had started after her escape.

Coll and Winnag met her. Her family had gone.

"I've met him," she whispered, but she had

no time to say any more. Slave women led her away, washed her and dressed her once again in gorgeous clothes and jewels.

The sun reddened behind dark hills and bare trees. The moon appeared in the sky. All round the enclosure people touched lucky things and said charms against the power of the dead, but Bel picked up her wooden cross and didn't scream or try to run away as the priests led her to the Maiden's Ring.

The old stones loomed out of the darkening glen. Torches were lit. Up in the High Fort Bel guessed that Derril and his friends would be keeping Samhain Feast, mixing old ways with the new, praying before crosses carved on stone, but casting rings into water, trying to foretell the future.

Bel tried to whisper Columba's prayer to herself, but her heart thumped so hard inside her embroidered dress that the words wouldn't come out of her dry lips. Then she heard chanting. Voices rose and fell on the air like the tide. The sound came from the very heart of the stone circle as singing figures wove their way in and out of the old stones. The stones stood very still, silent as ever, but the procession of singing people, each one holding torches, moved on and on.

"They remind me of Winnag's story about Sel and Sula," thought Bel. "Sel sang, while Sula searched for brambles. Her song showed Sula the way, Winnag said. But then Sel fell asleep and the fire went out. These singers aren't going to sleep, and they've brought torch light with them. How bright the flames are! Bright and friendly too. Light is like laughter — it drives the dark away. But what will Wyn and the other priests think? What will they do?"

They didn't seem to be able to do anything except stand and stare at the wavering torches which filled Samhain dusk with dancing light.

And now the sound of singing was so loud that Bel could hear the words.

"They're singing Columba's prayer! And there is Columba! And there are so many, many people. I think everyone in the glen except the king himself has come here tonight."

And so it seemed, as, holding a wooden cross high, Columba led the torch-lit procession around the stones. There were warriors from the High Fort, poets and singers, noblewomen and their maids, mothers and children.

"There's Coll! And that man beside him must be his friend, the monk Eochdair." And now Coll had seen her too and waved to her, while Eochdair looking across at Bel lifted his right hand and made the shape of a cross towards her.

Bel waved back. "I'm not afraid now," she thought. "No one's afraid. And there is my family, and Derril's come too." She smiled and waved again and again: to her parents and her little sisters; to Derril who walked tall and proud among the warriors.

And still the singing went on, echoing among

the stones; and now it seemed as though the first stars had come out to hear the sound.

"No wonder," thought Bel. "I'm glad you've come out, stars, even though there aren't many of you yet. The last time I saw you, I remembered Columba's prayer and now everyone in the glen is singing it."

Everyone except Wyn and the priests. They drew closer together and Bel knew that they were the ones who felt afraid.

"They never expected to see so many people on Columba's side," thought Bel, as the procession paused for Columba to speak to the priests.

"Peace be with you,"

Wyn found his voice at last. "Get out of our way," he ordered. "Our gods demand their sacrifice."

"It has already been made by the King of Kings himself," said Columba calmly.

Wyn's jewelled fingers flashed in the torchlight. He spread his hands wide. Bel saw in his eyes the faraway look she had noticed before, when he told her she was favoured and gifted. "He is trying to bend Columba's will to his own," she thought.

"There is no King of Kings in this glen," Wyn said, and repeated loudly: "No King of Kings."

Columba paid no attention to Wyn's loud voice.

"The King of Kings has made the sacrifice," he repeated "And the King in the High Fort has forbidden you to shed human blood any more."

Wyn's eyes lost their faraway look. His hands dropped to his sides, but his voice was scornful as he answered, "The King in the High Fort will never interfere with the priests in the Ring."

"Scornful you may be," said Columba, "but in the Name of the King of Kings whom I serve I tell you again, you are forbidden to kill this girl you stole from her family and kept unwillingly captive."

Columba and his monks moved closer. The whole procession stopped singing and gathered around them.

"Do not move one step further, priests of the Ring," said Columba. "There is to be no sacrifice."

"Blood must be shed, however," Wyn said, trying to speak evenly. "There has been sickness in the glen all summer."

Columba turned to the monks in their long tunics and cloaks of undyed wool. "My soul-brothers and servants of Christ, is there any sickness now?" he asked.

"No," said one of the monks, and Bel wondered if he could be Coll's friend, Eochdair, "we worked all summer with herbs and prayers. No one is ill now."

"Then we must sing the praises of God our Healer," said Columba and the whole procession moved forward again, circling the stones.

And now it seemed as if the sea itself had surged forward and, though Wyn and the priests shouted orders, neither they nor their slaves could move against all the people who surrounded the stones, singing loud praises, filling the glen with this new music. Round and round and round the stones walked this endless procession, and Wyn and his priests stood dumbfounded, as helpless as if Columba had turned them into rocks on a seashore: rocks against which churning waves pounded.

And now Columba was passing once more, and in full view of them all he held out his hand to Bel and said to her, "Little maid, will you come?"

"Oh, yes," she said, gladly and let herself be swept forward into the swaying, singing torch-lit lines of people. She lost sight of the priests as the crowd caught her up into its midst. Slowly she walked with them round and round the stones.

8

I WILL MAKE THE
WATER SWEET

The singing and walking around the stones went on and on. At some point in the night Coll must have stolen away from the priests and their slaves because there he was suddenly, walking at Bel's side, singing with the rest. Once Bel noticed Winnag standing beyond the torch-flare, watching without moving. Then they stood still and Columba prayed, hands held high to the starry sky.

Owls hooted, but no one felt afraid.

Bel remembered how she had begged the stones to help her mother get well again.

"The stones are deaf and dumb," she thought. "Columba's prayer has more power."

And then she noticed that the priests had disappeared. Silently, in twos and threes, as the unbroken procession surrounded the stones, blocking their way, they had simply melted away. They would make their sacrifice in their way, offering a calf or deer and, perhaps, pouring out its blood, but Bel was safe.

She turned to Coll. "They've gone, and I'm safe. Oh, Coll, I'm not going to die."

He nodded. "Columba turned them to stone," he said.

"That's what I thought too," said Bel. "They stood so still. They didn't know what to do, but they didn't dare break through the crowd and move into the Ring, although Wyn tried to bend Columba to his will. I saw him."

"I saw him too," said Coll, and shivered. "We're both free of him now, Bel."

"Both of us?"

"Yes, I'm never going back to that Temple again."

"What will you do instead?"

"I shall ask Columba to make me one of his monks," answered Coll.

And now people, noticing that the priests had gone, gathered closer to Columba.

"Go back to your homes in peace," he told them, "and remember this — we need no sacrifice or Temple because Christ our King prays for us to his most High Father." He stretched out his hands and sang:

I do not fear owl or crow
Nor do I utter charms against ill chance:
My love, my defence is my Christ and my God.

"Hold to this faith and God will guard you as he has guarded this child tonight," Columba told the people of the glen. And in front of them all he led Bel back to her parents.

"It was Bel's love for you which led her to make

an offering in the Ring," he said to her mother. "Let her follow her heart's desire, and do not fear ill luck any more." And to her father he added, "Let Bel lead you back into the good ways you knew once. Now go home and sleep."

But Bel said, "Please, Columba, will you look after Coll. He's run away from Wyn. He doesn't want to belong to the priests any more."

Columba nodded. Beneath his high forehead, shaved of its hair, his face was drawn and tired. His shoulders sagged. "The work goes on and on," he said, and then he smiled. "Don't be afraid, Bel. Coll is already a servant of our Christ and his safety is sure."

Bel thanked him, and so did her parents. They wanted to give Columba presents, some of the costly things the priests had brought when they had taken Bel away, but he refused. "Keep what you need," he said, "and share the rest with the poor in the glen." Yet Bel knew from what the monk Eochdair told Coll that Columba ate very little, and slept on the bare earth with a stone for a pillow, and his only possession was a book containing words from the Bible which he had copied out himself.

Stumbling with tiredness, Bel went home with her parents to her own fireside. Her father carried a sleeping Genann on his shoulders. Her mother half-carried, half-coaxed Mooreen along. Derril, who had permission to sleep at home that night, and Bel took Elir between them. Derril's dog Swift, now fully grown, bounded to meet them as soon as they got home. He recognized Bel and gave her a great welcome. They wrapped the little girls in woven rugs but, before they themselves lay down, Bel's father said, "When I was small my mother, good and kindly as she always was, prayed a prayer of blessing on our house and our hearth. And as Columba reminded us, we should do the same."

So Bel sang the prayer which had comforted her when she had felt so lonely and homesick:

These are the Three Guarding ones:
Father, Spirit and the Son.
Be ever with us, Lord we pray,
each noon, each dark, each break of day.

And her father and mother and Derril sang with her.

That night Bel fell asleep by her own fireside, safe and free from worry and fear, while out in the glen, in small huts they had woven out of willow, Columba and his monks sang their night prayers. Coll was with them, singing too, knowing that next day Columba was going to plead with Wyn on his behalf and beg the priest to set the slave-boy free.

When Bel next met Coll he wore a cloak of undyed wool and had no iron collar round his neck, but Bel couldn't ask him about it, because there was another ceremony taking place, and she was part of it.

They were all at the burn. It was a day in late

November. The rowans had lost their leaves, and although the sun shone there was no warmth at all in it.

Bel and her family were wearing their best clothes, because today Columba was coming to baptize them; and, because of everything that had happened at the Maiden's Ring, a great crowd had turned up, and everyone was wearing their finest clothes. Warriors from the High Fort came and there was even one of the royal princes there, to show everyone how important King Connail thought it that there were to be no more sacrifices during the old feasts in the glen.

"We will keep the feasts," the king had said, "but we will keep them with prayers and holy songs, just as Columba has taught us."

Because it was late in the year and the water was cold, Columba was careful to scoop up only a little water into a silver basin which he warmed between his hands before sprinkling just a few drops over the heads of the men, women and children he baptized.

When it was Bel's turn she stood very still and tried not to blink away the water which trickled into her eyes and dripped on to her lips. She licked it away amidst the prayers and singing and recalled her questions: why was burn water sweet and why was there so much death in the glen?

She still didn't know all the answers, but she knew how close to death she had been.

"The sacrifice has already been made by the King of Kings himself," Columba had said. Bel remembered his words as Columba bent over her and made the shape of a cross on her forehead. She remembered how Coll had looked at his baptism, quiet and glad as though nothing hurt him any more, not even his iron collar. "And he's not wearing it now," thought Bel. "Columba must have rescued him from Wyn."

She clambered up the bank and stood beside her family.

"Unlucky things don't matter any more," she whispered to her mother who shook her head.

"I think they still matter," she said, "but prayer matters more. I know that because I have my daughter safe and sound even though the baby died."

Bel nodded. "If the baby hadn't died I should never have gone to the stone circle to pray," she thought. Deep within her she sensed that her unnamed, unknown brother, dead before he had even lived, mattered too. She sensed that there had been a meaning in it all which she could barely guess at.

The wind blew across the glen. Bel shivered and looked round, and was pleased to catch sight of Winnag, wrapped warmly in a cloak her mother had made from the cloth the priests had given them.

"I'm glad Winnag's here," thought Bel. "As soon as I can I'll go across and speak to her."

But there was no time just then, for Columba was speaking.

"Why do we baptize in ordinary water, sweet

and clear as it is?" he asked. "We use it because God the kindly Father cares so much for his creatures that he has given us water to drink. 'I will make the water sweet and clear,' said the Father all-wise in his hall of light beyond the breaking waves of the farthest sea, 'so that life will be healthy and pure on the earth.' For the Father of Healing," explained Columba, "is loving and good. And so we use the good things which the Lord of our love has made for us, not the wine of festivity, or the fiery spirits of drunkenness, but pure sweet water such as Mary would have carried each day from the village well, Jesus himself helping her, never too proud to disdain the simplest task.

"But the water itself, the good, clear water which tastes of the very sweetness of life, when we use it in baptism becomes a gate to a garden beyond, a wonderful garden indeed," Columba went on with a smile. "So listen now and try to understand. What would happen if, when you sow your corn and your barley, the seeds refused to fall into the earth out of sight?"

"We wouldn't have any corn at harvest time," someone in the crowd answered and the others listening agreed.

"We wouldn't have any bread," added Winnag, who had worked her way from the edge of the crowd to stand as close as she could beside Columba and hear what he said.

"And we should starve," Columba himself finished. "But within us we each have a grain of

94

corn: our own hearts and wills. That is the thing which makes each of us what we are. We must let this grain fall into Christ so that he may live his life in us. This is a very great mystery, but I understood it well when I turned my back on my homeland and set sail across the sea. So now I tell you that in baptism we say, 'I am about to enter the garden of life because I am Christ's and no one else's.' I say this, I who have killed kings and marched with great armies, because I have given myself into the hands of the King of Kings."

"Do you understand what he's saying?" Wnaing whispered, nudging Bel.

"I'm not sure,' she returned.

"He's saying burn water is sweet because God who made it is good. And he's saying the same as I told you already that Corn Maiden has to die to feed the earth."

"Only for Columba it's Christ and not Corn Maiden," Bel reminded the old woman, "and it is for me too," she added.

"I know it is, dearie," said Winnag, "and I'm glad, for it was the Christ of Columba who snatched you from death in the Maiden's Ring."

"Aren't you going to be baptized too, Winnag?" asked Bel.

The old woman shook her head. "No, dearie, it's not part of my ways. I'm too old for new things, but you must pray for your Bright Christ for me just the same.'

Bel nodded, but now she wanted to sing with everyone else in the glen. She wanted to sing because Columba, who had once marched with powerful armies, had come over the sea to Dalriada; because Coll didn't have an iron collar round his neck any more, and because her mother wasn't afraid of ill-luck (or at least knew how she could guard against it). Most of all she wanted to sing because she was alive, standing here with her family beside the tumbling burn with the wind in her hair and because she could run, when the singing and ceremony were done, over the hill where shy red deer bounded faster than she.

And so Bel sang praises beside the swift clear water of the burn, and her family and Columba and his monks and Coll and the people of the glen sang too. Afterwards there was feasting in the High Fort with Columba seated beside King Connail.

So Bel didn't have time to run over the hills that day, but she stood on the rocks which surrounded the Fort and felt the wind blow through her hair, while Coll stood beside her in his cloak of undyed wool and told her his story.

"I have no family at all," he said. "My mother died when I was born and my father was drowned when he was out fishing one winter. Relatives looked after me. They found me a foster-father, but he was very poor and when I was seven he sold me to the priests in the temple in exchange for barley."

"How did you feel?" said Bel.

"Very bad," said Coll, "but there was no one to

tell. No one even wanted to know how I felt, until one day a girl touched the iron collar round my neck. She noticed the scars it made and asked if it hurt."

"Did no one else wonder?" asked Bel.

"Who was there to wonder — or even notice?" said Coll. "I shall never forget what your question did for me, Bel. I think it's the most important question there is."

"What is?" interrupted Bel.

"To ask someone with an injury how badly it hurts," said Coll. "A slave's collar is a kind of injury after all," he added.

"And now you don't wear one any more," said Bel. "Does your neck still hurt, Coll? You've got a lot of scars."

He fingered his neck. "They'll fade," he said. "No, it doesn't hurt, Bel, nothing hurts now."

"That's good," said Bel, and then she asked, "How did you get free, Coll? I haven't heard that part of your story. Did Columba buy you from Wyn — although he doesn't have any gold or fine things, does he?"

Coll shook his head. "I don't know how he managed it. Only by prayer and going without even the little food he does eat. At least, that's what Eochdair said. Prayer and fasting are what they use against evil. Nothing else. I'm their servant now. I help prepare their food, but one of the brothers is teaching me to read and when I go to Columba's island I shall learn to write too, and then I'll be able to copy out the Scriptures."

"I'd rather listen to stories," said Bel. "I don't know if I agree with reading and writing, Coll."

"But it's important to be able to read," said Coll. "Then you don't need to rely on other people to tell you things. You can find out the answers for yourself."

"My mother says I ask too many questions," said Bel. "She says it's not always wise to ask so much."

"It's because of your questions that you came out for rowan blossom isn't it?" Coll reminded her. "Winnag told me that when we looked after you in the enclosure. So you see, if you hadn't we should never have met. Never stop asking questions, Bel."

"No, I shan't," Bel said. "it's part of being me, I think, even if it lands me in trouble," she added with a sigh. "So you're going away to Columba's island? I'm glad for you, but I shall miss you, Coll."

"I'll miss you too," Coll said, "but I won't be going yet, not until spring, I think."

"What will you do, besides copying out the Scriptures?" asked Bel.

"Pray and sing God's praises," said Coll, "and look after people who come to the island. I don't know what else. I might travel too, as Columba has done."

"While I stay on in the glen," Bel said. "I don't mind though. I belong here, just as Winnag does. I shouldn't like to live anywhere else." She leant over the ramparts of the Fort and pointed across

98

the glen. "Look how far you can see, Coll, but you'll be travelling further than that."

"And you'll be staying here. Can you see your homestead from here?" Coll asked.

"Yes, it's over there," Bel pointed, "but you know, whether we stay or go we've both shared something special in this glen."

Coll nodded his agreement.

"Come on, Coll," Bel said, "we're missing all the food and drink inside the Hall."

"And the celebration," Coll added, following Bel back into the King's Hall. "After all, today's a really important day, and we've got to celebrate your baptism."

"Not only that," Bel thought, but she didn't say it aloud in case Coll thought she was silly, that they had to celebrate because burn water, even in November, tasted sweet and life was good in the glen where the red deer ran.

9

"LARKSONG AND A GOOD STORY"

The next day high winds howled across the glen, whirling the last tattered leaves from shivering trees. People had bad colds and sniffed and coughed and sneezed, walking bent double against the wind on their way across the glen.

Bel, who loved wild weather, ran up the hill. The wind whipped her hair across her face and tossed it out behind her. It shook the branches of the trees and made wild music in the heart of the woods. Bel paused for breath, struggling to keep her balance. From her vantage point high up the hill she could glimpse the glimmer of the sea.

"Soon Coll will set sail across the sea to Columba's island," she thought, trying to imagine how his life would be; a gentle life, it might seem, of holiness and prayer into which the gale of God's love would rush. And there would be battles and conflicts too, which, like Columba, he would fight without sword or spear: battles against old gods and powers, but battles within his own heart too, of that Bel felt suddenly sure.

Into the rush and fury of the wind Bel prayed for her friend. "Guard Coll always," she begged.

The short day was ending in a flash of crimson, but the wind was as strong as ever. Bel started home, but decided to make a detour past Winnag's house.

A gust of wind nearly lifted her off her feet. Dirt blew into her eyes, and then she noticed that Winnag's roof had blown away in the strong winds.

Bel stared. How long had Winnag been left at the mercy of the weather?

She started to run towards the poor hut, shouting the old woman's name, but the wind carried her voice away.

"Winnag, can you hear me? Win-nag!" she called, cupping her hands around her mouth, but there was no answer, nor any sign of life in the ruined hut.

The fire was out, although Winnag's cooking pot still swung from a bare rafter. Bel looked up at the darkening sky. The first star shone right into the empty hut. An owl hooted from the hill. Bel shivered. "Owls belong to starlight and the dark," she thought, "but people need shelter." And she could only hope that Winnag had found somewhere safe to spend the night.

"I'd better go home, or else they'll all be worried," she thought, and indeed, hardly had she started off for home when she met Derril, out searching for her with a flaming pinewood torch held high above him, and his dog Swift at his heels.

"I thought I'd find you here," he greeted her, as Swift bounded to Bel with an enthusiastic welcome.

"I was looking for Winnag," Bel explained, patting Swift. "Her hut's in ruins. The roof's right off but there's no sign of her anywhere. I hope she's safe."

"Winnag's fine," Derril said. "if you come on home now you'll see her sitting at our fireside."

"Winnag? At our fireside?"

"Mother made barley broth," Derril explained.

Bel nodded. "I should know," she interrupted, "I chopped up the vegetables and ground the herbs."

"Well, she made a huge pot. 'We can't eat all this ourselves,' she said, and then someone, I think it was Elir, remembered that Columba told us to share things we didn't need. We thought about Winnag. You'd gone out, so I got sent down with the soup. I arrived just in time to see her roof — or what was left of it, blow right off."

"So did she agree to come home with you?" asked Bel.

"Not at once. She took quite a lot of persuading, but you can't sleep in a house without a roof . . ." Derril said, shielding his torch from a gust of wind as they went into the house. Bel went in, feeling quite shy at the sight of Winnag as her family's guest.

"Here you are now," the old woman said from

the fireside. "Darkness is always a good shepherd, gathering bairns and birds and beasts safely into their own folds."

Her knotted old fingers were busy as she spoke. She was doing a job Bel hated: teasing out wool to make it ready for spinning.

"I was out at your house looking for you," Bel explained.

Winnag smiled. "That was kind of you Bel," she said.

Bel's mother looked up from the cooking pot. "Winnag will stay with us until we've managed to make her a new roof," she said. "And so far her fingers haven't stopped working, and she's been busy telling stories too. How do you know so many stories, Winnag?" she asked.

"I'm old and poor, without a family of my own. I weave words to while my days away," Winnag said. "But they've not kept me warm or safe from the winter winds. Words are poor things, after all," she added, and now Bel lost her shyness.

"I think words are wonderful," she said, "when they're properly used, that is!"

"Now what does that mean, 'properly used'?" asked Winnag, teasing and pulling her wool into webs.

"Used in stories," Bel explained, "the way you use them, Winnag, or used in prayer the way Columba does."

She sat beside Winnag and played idly with the puffs of teased out wool. "Coll is going to write words," she said. "He will spread them on parchment and they'll lie trapped between leather covers. I don't think you should do that to words."

Elir was listening. "Why not, Bel?" she asked.

"Listen to the child with her questions! You'll make her as bad as you are!" Bel's mother sighed.

"I think words belong in the open, like stones or the wind," Bel said. "Like songs too. You can't hear the sound of words when they line up across a page. But Coll says that if you read books you don't have to keep asking people to answer your questions. You can find out the answers yourself."

"First it was iron swords which changed the old ways of the glen," said Winnag. "Now it's barefoot monks with feather pens. Perhaps Columba himself will tell us one day why he spends so much time making shapes in ink on parchment. But one thing's certain. You can never undo what's been done or go back on something once it's been begun. My own people had to learn that truth when they fled into mounds from naked iron swords."

Bel glanced anxiously across at her mother, certain that she would think this was an unlucky thing to say. But her mother was busy setting a large horn ladle beside the soup.

"Come and eat," she said.

And now from his side of the fire Bel's father spoke. "Winnag, you have come to our fire at our request, and there's no praise to us, for it's a pitiful thing to refuse shelter to anyone, friend or stranger."

Winnag replied, "There is much praise to you, however, for I am Winnag of this glen and therefore no stranger; yet neither am I your friend, for your people conquered mine, and there has never been any love between us."

Perhaps Winnag meant well and wanted to praise Bel's family for offering hospitality to someone like her, whom they had never welcomed or trusted, but Bel felt the atmosphere grow tense.

"Why did Winnag remind them of all the old hurts?" thought Bel. "She said to me once there was no more enmity between us."

But it seemed grown-ups can enjoy the company of a child from another race and still quarrel with one another, a quarrelling that is worse than the tiffs and fighting of children who soon make friends again. Her father turned an angry face away from the old woman. Her mother paused in the very act of handing Winnag the ladle full of soup.

"Why can't they understand one another?" Bel thought. "Why do they put up these barriers between one another. Winnag welcomed me into her hut. She made me her Midsummer Lady. She even spoke to Columba about me, and told me the story of the poor friendless woman who had nothing in the world except the one little calf which cruel men stole."

Yet Bel knew that if she intervened now and

reminded her parents how Winnag had come to the priests' enclosure and looked after her, coaxing her back into the land of the living from homesickness and despair, it would only make things worse.

"You can't trust these people," her mother was saying, while soup steamed from the ladle. "They would sell you for thirty bars of silver, no not even that, for thirty beads of common glass!"

Winnag said, "Better a soup of nettles under the ragged moon than meat at a fireside where both are grudged."

There was a terrible silence. Offence had been given and taken. Winnag had started it, and her mother had spoken words which had pierced Bel's heart like the iron swords which had conquered Winnag's people long before.

"I can't bear it," thought Bel, watching Winnag get stiffly to her feet, but there seemed nothing she could do.

"Bel began all this," her mother went on. "She visited you secretly. Oh yes, Bel, I could tell from the sayings and stories you brought home where you'd been. And all our mischance followed. My baby boy died. You killed him, old woman," she said. "Your bad influence brought him dead into the world."

And now it was as bad as if there had been no songs of forgiveness and love at their baptism, no talk of the wheat which must fall into Christ, no mention of the Tree of Life at the heart of a garden. . . . Up on the hill, in the teeth of the wind

Bel had prayed for Coll. Why, oh why, had she not prayed for her family as well, and for Winnag whose withered face was rigid with anger?

"Iron swords and accusing words kill my people, but we have words too: words of blessing and words of ill," Winnag said.

"She's going to curse us," Bel thought, "and then she'll go outside into the storm without any supper or any shelter."

"Winnag!" she implored, but although the old woman's name was bursting her brain with the pleading she didn't know how to utter, it sounded no more than a whisper on her dry lips.

Winnag turned her head and so did her mother.

"Be quiet, Bel," her mother said. "My baby boy died," she repeated, and there was nothing Bel could say.

The wind howled around the homestead. Branches clattered from the trees and faintly in the distance they heard wolves howl. Swift pricked up his ears and growled.

"There's fear and hatred inside our house and that's worse than wolves," thought Bel, and now she prayed within herself, "Lord Jesus, drive them from our hearts."

The fire blazed brightly and the soup smelt good. Swift settled back to sleep.

"I'm hungry," Mooreen said, and the other little girls added, "So are we!"

"I'm hungry too," thought Bel, "but I don't

want to eat with all this hatred. Children can't do a thing when grown-ups quarrel."

Not even a child who has been chosen to be the Maiden and be sacrificed for the life of the glen; not even a child who has been the Midsummer Lady and stood barefoot on the bare earth; not even Corn Maiden . . . Helplessly Bel watched Winnag walk slowly towards the door.

And then she got to her feet and ran. She couldn't help it, even if her parents thought she was ridiculous, even if they were to punish her, perhaps even send her away. She couldn't let Winnag walk out into the winter night like this. She raced across to Winnag and blocked her way.

"Don't go, Winnag," she begged. "We want you in our house. You're our friend."

"*Your* friend, Bel, not your family's, it seems," said Winnag.

"Yes, and my family's," declared Bel, fiercely. She turned towards her parents. "Have you forgotten Samhain Feast?" she demanded. "In the priest's enclosure I asked you to look after Winnag, because she had helped me when I was all alone and ill."

Her mother and father looked at each other. Outside the wind sent rain driving against their house. They heard it drumming on the roof.

"This is no night to be outside," said Bel's father. "Winnag of the Old Ones, we have been hot-tempered and hasty, wrongly dwelling on old grievances when a new way of love has come to our glen." He left his place at the fireside and came over to the old woman. "Forgive us, Winnag, if you can, and be very welcome at our hearth."

Winnag's eyes filled with tears. "I never thought the day would come when a warrior of the king's clan would speak gently to me," she said. "A faith which asks forgiveness is stronger than swords or bitter words." She let Bel's father lead her back to the fire where Bel's mother held out the ladle freshly dipped into the hot soup for her.

That night there was rejoicing in Bel's house with laughter and talk and singing to drown the sound of the rain and the howling of the wolves. Winnag launched into her stories, and Elir and Genann listened wide-eyed while Mooreen fell asleep on her mother's knee and Bel served them all drinks made of apples and honey.

And at the end of the evening Winnag said, "I think perhaps it was good that all those things which came between us were said, otherwise they would have lingered unspoken and caused even more hurt. And now, listen, because once I promised Bel of the brave heart and kindly ways that I would tell her how and why the stories have grown up about the fairy blood in my people. The moment is right, so that there should be no more misunderstanding between us."

"Tell us, Winnag," Bel's mother said, "and then we must sleep."

"I'll be brief," promised Winnag, "and then we

shall sleep. Know then that a people may be conquered, as my people were, by iron swords and fighting men — and women too," she added, "but the ways, beliefs, songs and speech we learnt at our mothers' knees are harder than human blood to destroy. Stories are remembered when the lips which told them are stilled. And when the stories themselves disappear their memory lingers on. It's the faint echo of lost stories which tell of the fairy powers of my people. Now I cannot tell you, neither in the sun's circling nor the darkling of the world, whether those stories are true, but what I am saying is that a good story always tells of the true. No one knows the meanings of the carvings cut long ago into the stones which march in rings all over our glen, but if you listen carefully to the echoes of lost stories you will learn something true about the forgotten ways of the old people.

"Bel has listened," Winnag went on, "and she has understanding now which is not given to everyone. But she has listened too to Columba, the kingly one from Ireland with his warrior's heart and his dove's name, so now I shall call her Bel of the Bright Love, but still to me she is Corn Maiden who dances among the sharp knives of hatred and fear to reconcile her family and an old weary woman. For Bel's sake, for the sake of the love in her heart, Winnag wishes Bel's family well."

She stood up and, walking the way of the sun around the fire she went round them all, wishing them well.

"I walk the way of the sun's circling," she said. "May peace and joy walk with you always."

Perhaps it was just a trick of the firelight and the guttering flames of seal-fat lamps, but as she walked she seemed taller and queenly, and her rags seemed to float around her like thistledown. Her sparse hair thickened and her face became younger while her words had a lilt as though small flutes gave utterance and sounding.

"Walk well in our long glen into larksong and a good story," she said, smiling at Bel.

"Yes, Winnag," answered Bel, "for we're all part of a story which will carry us to halls of light where the larks keep on singing to honour our King."

But whether she actually said that, or just dreamt the words afterwards, dozing by the warm fire, she was never too sure. Perhaps it didn't matter anyway. The main thing was that they were safe from the wind, the rain and the wolves, and that peace and understanding had replaced the fear and hatred there had been in their house.

And in the days and weeks that followed they worked hard repairing Winnag's house, while the old woman sat at their fire teasing out wool which she later spun into thread for the family to use.

10

BRIGHTER THAN STARLIGHT

The winter gales swept the sky clean and chased the last leaves from the glen. Coll came along to help Bel's family make Winnag's new roof. He told them about another celebration soon to be held in the High Fort. "It is the Feast of Christmas," he said, "the birthday of the King of Kings, and Columba would like you all to come."

So that was something to look forward to, but meantime there was plenty of work to be done.

Bel told Coll how he had found Winnag's house in ruins with one star peeping through the storm-tossed clouds high above her head.

"Jesus was born in a barn with the stars shining through the roof," said Coll. "Columba will tell you all about it, and about the Night of the Gifts. But you're right, Bel, no one should have to sleep under a roof which lets the rain as well as starlight in, although Columba and his monks often spend whole nights under the stars."

So they worked hard piling turf and heather thatch on Winnag's rafters while the old woman sat spinning at their fireside.

And when Winnag's house was ready Coll came to join their celebration.

The old customs would have demanded a sacrifice. A black cock would have been considered especially lucky, but Winnag didn't want any blood shed on her doorstep.

"You must give this house your blessing, Coll of the praying hands," she said, and Bel was pleased. But Coll replied, "Bel, you and your family worked harder than me. I think you should all bless Winnag's house." And so they sang the hymn Bel had first heard at Coll's baptism.

These are the Three Guarding Ones:
Father, Spirit and the Son.
Be ever with us, Lord, we pray,
each noon, each dark, each break of day.

Bel had a present for Winnag: the little cross of rowan wood which Coll had given her.

"It means a lot to me," she said to Coll, "but I want Winnag to have it, and I'll tell you why when we're on our own."

Winnag was delighted with Bel's gift and they fixed the cross carefully above her door. Then they all ate bread made from the fine wheat flour the priests had given them, with meat and pieces of honeycomb.

Then, as the short winter day was coming to its early end, Bel and Coll left Winnag's house together. Without specially meaning to, they found themselves heading for the burn and the spot where they had first met.

"So Winnag and your family are friends now?" said Coll.

"Yes, at last, but there was a terrible time when they all misunderstood each other and said hurtful things. It was very bad, Coll. Then my father said sorry; but, oh, Coll, my mother said something which cut me in two when I heard it, and that's why I wanted to give Winnag your cross. She said, about Winnag you know, 'You can't trust *these people.*' *These people* ... the words seem so full of scorn. Do you know what I mean?"

Coll nodded. "It's the sort of thing people say all the time about you when you're a slave."

"I suppose they must do," Bel replied thoughtfully, then she rushed on, "and after that she said, 'They'd sell you for thirty silver bars, or not even that, for thirty beads of common glass'."

Coll looked at her, "Bel, doesn't she know that's what happened to our Lord? He was sold for thirty silver pence. Columba says that was the price of a thrall in those days."

"A thrall? Jesus? But he's the King of Kings."

"I know. I could hardly believe it at first." In the silence which fell between them they stared at the burn, running busily and noisily over the stones, feeding the long winding river with water until it finally emptied itself into the sea.

"I shall miss you when you go away to Columba's island," said Bel.

"I shall miss you too," Coll returned, "but I'll pray for you, Bel. Columba and the rest of the monks spent a lot of time praying," he went on. "Sometimes I join them, but, you know there are times when I can't help wondering what use it all is."

"That's what I wondered when I prayed to the stones, but I've never thought it since," said Bel. "Go on, Coll, about praying I mean."

"Well, I think prayer is a bit like the burn. Sometimes it's quite easy. It seems to flow along all by itself. Other times it's still and deep, but there are times when it seems almost to dry up altogether."

"If it does that, there's drought and sickness," Bel reminded him.

"That's just it," said Coll, "but when the burn flows well everything in the glen goes well too — and that's good. Then in the end the water flows down to the sea."

"Which is huge and cold and salt and dangerous, but very, very beautiful," said Bel, remembering her talks with Winnag, and now the silence between them was drowned by the noisy burn.

"I shall have to go," said Coll, finally. "It's almost dark now. I'll see you at the Fort, Bel, and we'll keep the Christmas Feast together."

When the time came to celebrate the birthday of the King of Peace, Winnag stayed in her hut.

"I'm snug and warm here, thanks to you," she told Bel's family who called for her. "I'm too old to climb all the way up to the Fort."

"We'll help you, Winnag," said Bel, and Elir

115

put in, "It's the Time of Gifts," but Winnag shook her head.

"You've given me many good gifts," said Winnag, "not least your friendship. Now, off you go. Tell Coll of the Gentle Heart to pray for me."

They set off, armed with torches and lanterns beneath a darkening sky and hurried across the moorland to the High Fort, where Columba was waiting for them, and for all the people of the glen who had left their firesides to keep the Feast.

"This is the time of year when the nights are longest," Columba said. "It's good that you've come here so that we can remember that Christ has come like a light in the dark."

He led the way into the Fort. The monks followed, their feet shod in rough leather, but Coll walked ahead of Columba, carrying a wooden cross. Then King Connail of Dalriada laid his crown aside and walked behind Columba and the cross-bearer who had been a thrall.

"It is the Night of Gifts," sang Columba. His fine voice echoed all through the Hall, among flaring torches, roaring fires, crowds of brightly dressed people, sweating cooks and scurrying thralls.

"It is the night when Christ was born. It is the birth of love," sang the monks.

Then Columba turned to speak to the people and they gathered close to hear him, though the cooks still kept an anxious eye on the steaming pots.

"May the King whose Kingdom is brighter than starlight continually pour out upon you the love of his heart," said Columba. "Listen now, and I shall tell you what gifts we may offer our Lord.

"Kings bring the Christ-child gold, that is the love of our hearts, sweeter to him than sunbeams in summer's bright halls.

"Princesses bring linen, that is our prayer, more pleasing to this baby than gossamer or thistledown.

"Children bring him skylarks, that is our praise, more melodious in his ears than the singing of snow-white swans. These are the gifts, but above all we must come to the step of his throne with his holy name upon our lips. And what is this throne of his? It is the poorest throne of all: a cradle in a trough where beasts come to eat. Now nothing is too mean or poor because our God has come among us at a time of great dark and he has brought us light."

Then the feasting began, amidst music and laughter, to be followed by the telling of stories, blessings and songs. In the speach of the people of her own glen Bel would hear (and re-tell the tale afterwards to Winnag) how Mary wandered with mist in her hair over moorland and hillside carrying the Son of God in her arms. She had neither food nor shelter, but the shield of God was with her, and hospitable people fed the homeless mother and warmed her child at their own hearthsides.

117

But before the story time started Bel slipped away from the bright hall and noisy feasting to stand alone beneath a swirl of stars. The cold night cooled her cheeks. She pulled her thin woollen cloak closer and stared up at the stars until their dazzle seemed to blind her.

"The Kingdom which is brighter than starlight has come to our glen," she thought.

She heard footsteps and there stood Columba, close to the sacred stone where kings of Dalriada were ceremoniously crowned.

Bel shrank back, planning to tiptoe away, but Columba seemed as always able to sense someone there. He turned and smiled. "Bel of the clear spirit, sweet as the laughing burn, would you like to hear a story?" he asked.

"Oh yes," replied Bel, but she was shivering. Columba at once placed his cloak of plainest undyed wool over her shoulders.

"A prince once lived with his Father in a stronghold of splendour," said Columba, "but to win peace for the King's poorest people he left his bed of soft down and his Father's Hall, where he was loved and respected. He made his home with a poor woman in a remote glen and served her and her household until he grew into manhood. Then he set out to walk the dusty roads of his Father's kingdom. Out in the wind and weather his skin grew brown like the hide of a deer and, like a deer in a snare, his enemies finally brought him to bay. They baited and cruelly used him, placing about his brows a crown knotty as a deer's broken antlers, which caused him much pain in all the distress of death. But, Bel, beside the running water of your homestead where you call to the escaping deer, there comes, thirsting for sweet burn water, the noblest and most kingly One, pierced with death-dealing spears for the healing of our hurts. Follow him without failing or fear for he will lead you to a hall of milk-white ivory where all our stories will one day find a happy end," Columba finished.

Into Bel's mind came a picture: a white stag lowered golden antlers to drink the tumbling water of her burn, and when he lifted his head a cross gleamed between the shining horns. Beneath them his eyes were filled with laughter which melted Bel's heart.

"I can't bear it," she whispered. "It's too beautiful for me . . . and now he's gone. He's gone!" she lamented, her face buried in Columba's rough cloak. "Did you see him, Columba?" she asked.

"No, Bel, dear heart, that seeing was for you alone, for the flame of love burns brightly in your heart and you have stood in dangerous places. But the Bright Christ of your love will always be with you as you walk the hillsides of home," he promised, and with those words he led her back to the firelit hall where the king's minstrels and poets were about to begin their songs. Bel sat with her family and Coll came and joined them.

"I've made you another cross, Bel, of birchwood for purity and grace," he said, giving it to her, and in return she gave him a bag she had woven for him, "to carry your parchments and pens," she explained, "though I still think you shouldn't trap words behind black lines of ink!"

All over the Hall people were exchanging presents, and bread was lifted from hot stones and shared around while stories were told. Then the people of the glen set off homewards beneath the stars, singing as they went in a group.

As they came near Winnag's hut Bel broke away, holding her torch high, and laid barley bannocks from the king's fireside, carefully wrapped, inside Winnag's door.

"She'll find them in the morning and then I'll tell her all about our feast," she explained to her family as they turned into their own house, dropping a deerskin curtain across the downpour of stars which flooded their glen.

Also from Lion Publishing

UNDER THE GOLDEN THRONE

Ralph Batten

"Under the golden throne, in the palace of the High King, lay Shamar, the one and only dog of Patria. Slowly he yawned and opened a big, brown eye . . ."

In the seven tales of Shamar the dog, we meet a wealth of comic characters including the self-important Prime Minister of Patria, the fussy Chancellor of the Exchequer and the dignified Derel the Wise. And, of course, the delightfully stupid Seven Knights of the Realm.

Each story tells of an adventure of Shamar the dog and his beloved master, the High King of Patria. And at the end of each story, Shamar settles down under the golden throne and sleeps. And as he sleeps, he dreams a dream . . .

IBSN 0 85648 780 5

IN THE KINGDOM OF THE CARPET DRAGON

Ralph Batten

Princess Anah is surprised by her royal
birthday gift. It is nothing more than a
stone on a golden chain. But this ordinary-
looking stone can be used to change
anything in the Kingdom of the Carpet
Dragon. It is up to the princess to discover
what needs changing, and when, and
how . . .

Accompanied by her lovable, loyal and
remarkably clumsy pet dragon, Doxa, the
princess sets out on her quest — with some
surprising results.

ISBN 0 7459 1533 7

PANGUR BÁN, THE WHITE CAT

Fay Sampson

The princess Finnglas is in the deadly grip of the evil Sea Monster, deep down in the mysterious underwater kingdom of the Sea Witch. And Niall has been bewitched by the mermaids.

Pangur Bán, the white cat, is desperate. He must rescue them — but how can he free them from the enchantment?

Only Arthmael can do it. But who is Arthmael? Where is he? Can Pangur find him in time?

Shortlisted for the *Guardian* Children's Fiction Award in 1984, this is the second book about Finnglas and her friends.

ISBN 0 85648 580 2

FINNGLAS OF THE HORSES

Fay Sampson

Dangers, surprises and unexpected happiness lie ahead for the princess Finnglas as she sets out to find her beloved horse, Melisant.

For her companions, Niall and Pangur Bán, the white cat, this desperate quest is an adventure they will never forget.

This is the third book about Finnglas and her friends.

ISBN 0 85648 899 2

DREAM-TELLER
The story of Joseph

Max Bolliger

"Whoever can tell me the meaning of my
dreams shall be richly rewarded,"
promises Pharaoh.

But none of the wise men, soothsayers or
prophets at the Egyptian court can explain
their king's mysterious and troublesome
dreams. In desperation he turns to Joseph,
one of his prisoners, for help. Can the
Hebrew slave live up to his reputation as
an interpreter of dreams and regain his
long-lost freedom?

Joseph, one of the best-known of Old
Testament heroes, is brought to life in this
action-packed retelling.

ISBN 0 7459 1345 8

KING'S CAPTIVE
The story of Daniel

Max Bolliger

Belshazzar's feast is brought to a standstill
when strange foreign words, written by an
invisible hand, suddenly appear on the
palace wall. What can they mean? The wise
men and scholars are baffled. Only Daniel,
an exile from Jerusalem, understands the
dreadful message. Will he dare tell the
wicked king of the doom and destruction
that the writing foretells?

An exciting retelling of the life of one of the
best-known of Old Testament prophets.

ISBN 0 7459 1344 X

More stories from LION PUBLISHING for you to enjoy: